SHARDS OF BETRAYAL

A LANIE PRICE MYSTERY

PERSIA WALKER

BLOOD VINTAGE

For Margaret, Kathleen and Gina

There's the truth you tell them. And the one you carry with you after they're gone.

ABOUT THIS BOOK

Filmmaker Seth Carter is a maverick whose latest project aims to bring authentic black stories to the silver screen. When reporter Lanie Price visits the set, she uncovers a plot of sabotage threatening lives and the film's future. Seth's dream hangs by a thread.

Seth pleads with Lanie to keep the sabotage under wraps, plunging her into an ethical and professional quagmire that could ruin her career—and sever her relationship with the man she loves.

Step onto a movie set where dreams are made—and lives are shattered. *Shards of Betrayal* is a gripping noir tale of ambition, betrayal and the relentless pursuit of a dream in the vibrant yet perilous world of 1920s Harlem.

PROLOGUE

L et me tell you about Seth. He made films on a
shoestring and I mean the thinnest shoestring you've
ever seen. No fancy studios for Seth Carter—he shot in
friends' houses, abandoned offices, anywhere he could get
decent lighting for free. There's this staircase in some
buddy's house where he filmed half of *Soul Redemption*.
Why? Best light angles in town.

Seth rented his equipment by the day because that's all
he could afford. No retakes, minimal editing. Those flubbed
lines and misspelled credits you see in his films? They
stayed in because every penny counted.

His actors... well, that was always interesting. His wife,
Grace Lewis-Carter, was his leading lady in most films—and
let me tell you, she had real star quality. Grace could make
even the most amateur supporting cast look good. Seth had
a knack for making it all work somehow. He was always
hustling, always thinking three moves ahead. One morning
he dragged Grace out to some fancy white neighborhood
when nobody was home, just to get footage of her in front of

an elegant house. Another time, he borrowed some society lady's fur coat while she was in a meeting—had Grace wear it for a quick scene. That was Seth all over—resourceful to the bone.

The man taught himself everything about filmmaking—each shot captured in stolen moments, each scene a patchwork of ingenuity and improvisation—but what he really understood was people. He'd go door to door selling his vision, just like he used to peddle his novels to white farmers and black communities down South. When he needed money for a film, he'd show up at theaters with his actors in tow, have them act out scenes right there in the manager's office. Hard to say no to that kind of showmanship.

Seth was pure electricity in person. Could charm the shoes off your feet while you were still wearing them. Sure, his company was always running on fumes financially, but his personality and non-stop hustle kept things afloat. He had to take money from white theater owners and investors —"angels," they called themselves—but Seth never lost control of his stories.

The stories themselves? That's where Seth and his younger half-brother, Clay, really shined. Clay Harper had a way with words, could spin out scripts that kept audiences on the edge of their seats. Between Clay's writing and Seth's vision, they tackled issues other filmmakers wouldn't touch —lynching, racial passing, prostitution, crime. They wove current events and controversial topics into plots that felt real, felt urgent.

Seth showed the complicated, messy stuff that sets black against black, the ironies and painful truths others avoided. His films weren't always pretty, but they were honest. While everyone else was trying to put on a good face, Seth was holding up a mirror to reality. Sometimes that mirror showed things people didn't want to see, but Seth never flinched. That was his power.

In the end, it turned out to be his curse too.

1

The Bronx was a furnace that July. Inside the warehouse, it felt even hotter. Air thick as wool. Hard to breathe through. Sweat pooled at the base of my spine the minute I stepped onto the movie set.

Didn't stop the crew. Black and white, they moved like gears in a well-oiled machine—grips hauling cables, costumers darting in to straighten a collar or reset a hem. The place smelled of sawdust, hairspray, greasepaint and nerves.

Somewhere in that blur, Seth Carter was directing his latest film.

I wasn't supposed to be there. I covered society for the *Chronicle*—teas, galas, scandals. But the regular film reporter was down with a bad cold. When Sam Delaney asked for a volunteer to interview Seth, I said yes.

Soul Redemption was already the talk of colored cinematic circles. A bold project, ambitious in scope, with a cast of complex, fully human colored characters. No maids. No comic relief. Seth meant to shatter the mold—and he just might do it.

I skirted a rack of costumes and nearly collided with a frazzled assistant carrying a tray of coffee. Somewhere behind the glare of lights and swarm of bodies, my interview waited.

The main filming area stretched out before me—a Harlem street scene, lovingly recreated. Storefronts lined a cobblestone path. A barbershop stood to one side, a jazz club interior on the other. On its stage, brass instruments caught the light. The craftsmanship was remarkable, all the more so because it was held together with spit and grit. Filmmaking on a shoestring. Raw. Unvarnished.

There—Seth. Conferring with a young man holding a clipboard near the jazz club set. Even in that chaos, he stood out. Towering, lean, in constant motion. He moved with purpose, his hands cutting through the air as he spoke. His white linen sleeves were rolled high, revealing forearms toughened from years of hauling gear.

"Mr. Carter," I called, stepping over a tangle of cords.

His gaze shifted to me, the briefest moment of recognition softening his intense focus.

"Ah, Mrs. Price." He extended a hand, his grip warm but distracted. "Right on time." Up close, the cracks showed. Drawn features. Dark circles under his eyes. The clipboard kid melted away, leaving us a pocket of quiet.

"Looks like you've got your hands full." I nodded to the whirlwind around us. "Impressive, what you've managed on limited means."

He smiled again, a polite reflex and shrugged. "Necessity breeds invention. We make do with what we have." His gaze slid to the cinematographer adjusting a dolly shot. "In this business, you learn to be creative or you don't survive."

"Those Remington spotlights must have cost a pretty penny."

"Found them in a warehouse in Jersey, if you can believe it." He smiled again—this time, genuine—but it passed quick. The tension didn't.

"So, Mr. Carter—"

"Seth."

"And I'm Lanie." I smiled. "So, do you still have time for that interview?"

His gaze shifted back to me and he nodded, half-apologetic. "Sure. Walk with me."

He led me through the controlled chaos, ducking cables, weaving past lights. The crew parted without being asked. Here and there, he paused to tweak a prop, murmur a note.

"Tell me about your crew."

He shrugged. "Nothing fancy. I hire the ones Hollywood left behind. Out-of-work gaffers, cameramen—folks who still believe in the work, even if the system doesn't believe in them."

"Non-professional actors too?"

"Friends, family, locals," he confirmed. "They're raw but real. It's cheaper, sure, but it's also about authenticity. My wife, Grace, helps balance the scales—she's got real training."

We climbed a narrow staircase. Each step creaked underfoot. The noise from the set faded behind us, muffled by walls and distance. At the top, Seth opened a door to what passed for an office—cramped, hot, tucked into a corner like someone's guilty secret.

A single window let in a sliver of late-afternoon light. Dust floated in it. Two desks stood shoulder to shoulder in the tight space. Both had typewriters, but that's where the similarity stopped. One was chaos—scripts, call sheets, scribbled notes and open envelopes stacked like a paper avalanche. The other was sterile. Not a paper out of place.

One sealed envelope in the inbox. A script, neatly typed and centered, sat like a tombstone in the outbox.

Seth dropped into a worn leather chair behind the first desk and nodded toward the seat across from him. The wood was scarred from use—arms worn smooth, corners dented. It had heard a lot.

"All right, let's get to it." He steepled his fingers. "What do you want to know?"

I sat, flipped open my notepad. "Let's start with representation. You're known for championing authentic portrayals of colored life on screen. Why does that matter so much to you?"

Obvious question. But obvious questions dig deep—if you let them.

He leaned back, hands still pressed together. "Because we've spent too long watching ourselves from the sidelines. Flat, easy roles—buffoons, mammies, savages. It's how they keep us small. They show a fraction of who we are and call it the whole. But we're more than that. We've got stories worth telling. Real ones."

A good quote. I jotted it down without looking away. "And *Soul Redemption?* Is that what this film is all about?"

"Absolutely. This one's personal. It digs into what's real —the pain, the promise. It's about two brothers: Cain and Abel Genesis—"

"You actually named them that?"

He gave a half-smile. "You know how it is. The Bible runs deep. Soon as folks hear those names, they think they know the ending. But that's the trap. In this story, the parents curse the children before the first frame. They name them, then vanish. We never even see them."

I nodded. "Go on."

"Cain's the elder. Hustler, survivor. Streets taught him

what school never did—how to take what he needs and leave the rest bleeding. He gets pulled into crime. Not because he wants to, but because the game's stacked and he's tired of losing.

"Abel's the opposite. Believer. Uplifts, educates, serves the community. The kind of man who thinks change starts with a book, not a bullet. He sees beauty even where there isn't any."

He paused. "The fight between them isn't just personal. It's everything we wrestle with—hope versus hunger. Morality against the grind. Abel—"

A sharp knock cut him off.

Seth looked annoyed, excused himself and called out, "Come in."

The door creaked open. A young man in thick work gloves leaned halfway in, sheepish.

"Sorry to interrupt, Mr. Carter. They're ready for the next scene. And, uh—Mr. Westbrook needs to talk to you about the lighting setup."

Seth glanced at me, then back at the grip. "Tell him I'll be there in ten."

The workman nodded quickly, his gaze darting to me before he backed and shut the door.

Seth settled back. "Now, where were we?"

"You were saying how the brothers' choices reflect the community."

"Right. Abel stands for the ideal—what we reach for. Cain's the world as it is. The hunger. The compromises."

"And in the end?"

"Well, let's just say they don't outrun the names they were given. They betray and nearly destroy one another. As much as they love one another, they cannot co-exist. One has to fall."

He paused, eyes shadowed. "The real question is—who betrayed whom? And why? Was it jealousy? Was it fear? Or was it love poisoned by jealousy?"

His voice dropped. "This is us. Our reality. We turn on each other. Not always for greed. But the damage is the same. We stab each other in the back, do at least as much damage as Mr. Charlie. In fact, we often do Mr. Charlie's work for him."

I caught that moment of hesitation in his eyes—that split second of regret. Like he'd said too much. Like he wanted to claw the words back. But he didn't.

And I respected him for that.

I tapped my pencil against the pad. "That kind of statement might rile some folks. Think colored audiences are ready for that kind of mirror—us turning on each other? A public airing of our dirty laundry?"

"Truth's not supposed to be comfortable," he said. "Change don't come wrapped in ribbons. It comes with cuts and bruises. People only learn when it costs them something."

"And white audiences? You care how they'll take it?"

He paused. "I care. Some folks say I shouldn't, but I do. I want them to see the truth, too. That we're not some monolith, all smiles and struggle. We've got divisions, tensions. Just like them. Betrayal doesn't come with a color—it's a human thing. If they're honest, they'll see that."

He shifted in his chair. "And then there's the other part."

"The box office."

"Yeah. That's the hard truth. More ticket sales means better films, better pay, steadier work for the crew. I can't afford to make just an 'artistic statement.' I've got to keep the lights on. That means reaching a wide audience—getting butts in seats."

"How do you plan to do that?"

He gave a half-shrug. "Talking to you is one way. Maybe you'll be kind. Or fair, at least."

I gave nothing away.

"Financing. Distribution. It's all rigged. But I'll work around it. I always have. Even if I've got to haul the reels from church basement to community halls, this picture's going to be seen."

He went quiet then, eyes on something past my shoulder. Then he squared his shoulders.

"It's not about doing it easy. It's about getting it done. About getting it seen. The world isn't kind to folks like us—but that doesn't mean we stop talking."

He smiled, grim and determined. "No one's going to hand it to us. We've got to take it."

I glanced down at my notes. He'd given me what I needed.

Seemed he thought so too.

"Well," he said, rising from the chair, "I've got a set to run."

I stood, slipped the notebook into my bag. "One last thing. Mind if I stay and watch for a bit? Get a better sense of your process?"

He hesitated—brief, but enough to catch. He hadn't expected that. His eyes went to the door, then back to me.

"Might not be the best idea. Things get a little ... chaotic out there. Don't want the crew losing focus."

The answer surprised me. And if I'm honest, rubbed the wrong way.

"Of course. But I can stay out of the way. I'm here to observe, not interfere."

He studied me a beat longer. Then gave a tight nod.

"All right. Follow me."

2

———

Seth moved between clusters of crew, me one step behind. His presence drew quiet nods. A grip called down from the rigging about light placement. A props man held up two nearly identical glasses. A cameraman gestured toward the rafters lost in shadow. Men worked the jazz club set—scarred tables, weathered bar, walls papered with peeling tobacco ads. The illusion of age held.

We threaded past cable snakes and light stands. Near the bar, two grips arranged tables to suggest a crowd while using half as many as a white studio would need. The sound of clinking glasses carried from somewhere—props department testing options for the scene. Seth's eyes never stopped moving, checking the space with the intensity of a man looking for something he hoped not to find.

Grace Carter stood by the bar, script in hand. I'd never met her but I knew her work—the haunting beauty in *Harlem Babylon*, the grieving war widow in *Crossroads of Fate*. She and Seth had met on *Babylon* and she'd starred in every one of his films since. Even in a simple day dress, she commanded attention. A young man—probably one of Seth's local finds—stood beside her, stiff with nerves.

"Watch how I move here." She demonstrated, her gesture fluid and precise. "Let the words follow the movement, not the other way around."

The boy nodded, wide-eyed. Grace had a reputation for nurturing green talent. Stories floated about her staying hours after wrap, helping extras get their steps right.

I excused myself from Seth and crossed over. Up close, her skin glowed honey-warm in the overhead heat. The light caught the gleam in her neatly waved hair.

She smiled. "Why, you're Lanie Price, aren't you?" She extended her hand. "Seth said a reporter was coming. Didn't say it'd be the *Chronicle's* best."

Behind her, Seth's gaze swept the rigging again. His fingers worked the edge of his rolled sleeve.

"Your husband was kind enough to invite me." I stepped carefully between cables . "Your scene in *Crossroads of Fate*, the letter-reading? I had to leave the theater. It cut straight to the heart."

Grace's smile dimmed, gentled. "Lots of women lost men in the war. I just thought about how they must've felt, getting that telegram." Her gaze slid to Seth. "That's what drives us. Telling the stories of the forgotten. Bringing their voices back."

A clean line. Polished. Delivered with just enough sincerity to make you believe it wasn't rehearsed.

Above us, metal groaned as someone adjusted a light. Seth's head snapped up at the sound. Grace noticed it, too—there was just a slight tightening around her eyes.

"Seth said this picture's different."

"Yes," she said, refocusing on me. "No stereotypes. These characters—they're as complex as we are." She touched the young actor's shoulder. "Show her what we were working on."

He straightened, ready, but then—

"Places, everyone!" Seth's voice cracked across the set.

Grace squeezed the boy's arm. "Next time." She rolled her shoulders, handed off her script. "Duty calls."

Seth gestured for me to take the folding chair beside his. "Grace, you ready?"

"Ready, Mr. Director."

Seth's smile was brief but real.

The warehouse fell silent save for the whir of the camera. Someone called, "Scene twelve, take three." The slate clacked.

Seth leaned forward, elbows to knees. "Action."

The transformation happened in an instant. The warm, gracious woman who'd greeted me vanished. The person who stood in her place had been hollowed by loss. Each movement resisted gravity. The young actor watched her, transfixed, then joined her in the scene. Their grief tangled like smoke.

"Hold that light steady," Seth said without turning.

"Got it, boss."

Shadow and light played across Grace's face, carving valleys beneath her cheekbones. Her hand trembled as she reached for a glass.

Metal scraped against metal somewhere in the rafters. Seth's fingers dug into his armrest. "Cut!" His voice carried. "Reset. We'll take it from the door."

The camera crew repositioned. Grace moved back to her mark. A grip climbed the ladder to adjust the spotlight. Seth scribbled a note in his script, but his attention kept darting upward.

"Everyone ready?" His voice carried to the rafters. "Let's make it count."

The warehouse hushed. The slate clacked again.

Grace stood frozen for a heartbeat, then moved like a woman underwater. Each gesture conveyed grief and pain. She reached the bar, let her fingers trail across its scarred surface. The young actor matched her rhythm, drawn into her gravity.

"The telegram came on a Tuesday." Her voice, though low, carried clearly. "I was hanging sheets in the yard."

The boy poured her drink. His hand shook."Miss Elizabeth—"

"Don't." Her shoulders curved inward, protecting an invisible wound. "Just ... don't."

Seth's frowned as he watched. Above, something creaked. His eyes flicked to the rigging, then back to the scene. A grip shifted his weight on the rigging and the metal groaned again.

"Cut." Seth sounded strained. "Reset the glasses." He stood, gaze fixed on the rafters. "And someone check that—"

A sharper scrape.

Seth moved to the edge of his chair, muscles coiled. His eyes tracked the grip adjusting the light above Grace. Sweat ran down the man's temple.

"Take five, everyone." Seth's fingers drummed against his thigh. "Wilkes, how's that connection looking?"

"Almost got it, Mr. Carter." Metal rasped against metal. The spotlight swayed.

Grace stayed in character, quietly running lines with the boy. Murmurs mixed with the hum of lamps, the shuffle of feet, the creak of the beams. Seth watched her. Then the rigging. Then her again. His hand kept drifting to his collar.

"All right, places." Seth massaged his chest. "From the telegram line."

Grace took her mark. The young actor lifted the bottle. The camera whirred.

Then came the sound—sharp, wrong, like a gunshot in church. A sharp cry. Wordless. Pure alarm.

The spotlight twisted free. Three hundred pounds of metal and glass swung once.

"Grace!" Seth lunged forward as the fixture plummeted toward his wife.

I caught the flash of her face, the mask of grief gone, replaced by real terror. Time stretched. Bodies scattered.

The crash hit like a cannon blast. Glass burst in all directions. Sound slammed the walls, then fell into a terrible quiet. Then came the delicate, terrible music of settling debris.

Silence.

Then Seth's voice, rough with fear: "Grace!"

She staggered, still on her feet, glass shards crunching under her shoes. "I'm all right."

When Seth reached her, his hands hovered over her shoulders, not quite touching. She caught his fingers, squeezed once, let go.

The crew gathered in knots, standing around, gaping at the shattered spotlight. Once Seth was satisfied that Grace was okay, he checked the boy who'd been standing beside her. Then it was on to his crew,.

No injuries.

Near the bar set, a heavyset cameraman with graying temples rolled a cigarette. "Third one this month." A young grip opened his mouth caught the older man's eye and stayed quiet.

A woman from wardrobe appeared with the first aid kit.

An electrician swept the glass into piles. Someone appeared with a large dolly. Two grips hefted the crushed frame.

Like choreography. No panic. No confusion.

Too smooth.

That wardrobe woman—too practiced. The broom in the electrician's hand—too ready. And that comment. *"Third one this month."*

I remembered how Seth kept eyeingthe rigging. The spotlights he'd bragged about. Warehouse finds from Jersey. That crew—Hollywood's left-behinds—his words, not mine.

Had he pushed too far? Cut too many corners?

Seth Carter breaking barriers was one thing. Gambling with lives was another.

"Seth? We need to talk."

He was with a grip. Looked up and read my face. Saw the questions forming, ones he most likely didn't want to answer.

He hesitated. Then gave a nod—quiet, resigned.

"Okay. Let's talk privately."

3

S eth led me back to the cluttered office and quickly shut the door behind us. The heat seemed even worse inside the small space. Another man was in there now, seated at the second desk, his legs stretched out before him. He strongly resembled Seth—had the same dark circles under his eyes—but he was younger, leaner. He looked up when we entered, eyes narrowing.

"Lanie, this is my brother, Clay. He's my script writer. I visualize, but he makes it real, puts it down on paper. Clay, this is the lady reporter I told you about."

Clay pushed himself up from the chair and crossed the room with a smooth, easy gait. He welcomed me with a warm smile and shook my hand. "Nice to meet you. Seth's been looking forward to talking to you."

"Has he? I—"

"Did something happen out there?" Clay asked, turning to Seth. "I thought I heard a crash."

"Yeah. There was—" Seth glanced at me and I was sure he changed what he was about to say, "an ... accident."

"Another spotlight?"

"Wait a minute," I said. "*Another one?*"

Seth shot Clay a look of annoyance, then turned back to me. "Yeah. We've uh ... had a run of bad luck."

Clay let out a short, derisive breath. "Luck's got nothing to do with it."

Seth gave another warning look, but it was too late.

I took a step closer. "What's going on?"

Seth pressed his lips tightly together.

"Seth?" I said.

He slowly raised his eyes to meet mine. Then he shook his head, said, "All right." He crossed his arms. "We're talking about equipment failing. Props breaking at the wrong time." A little shrug. "Nothing major. Just setbacks."

"Setbacks?" Clay cut in. "Jimmy almost got taken out by a runaway dolly and Lou burned his hand on a rigged prop. Setbacks don't almost kill people."

Seth didn't answer. Didn't look at me.

I waited. Let the silence do the work. Then: "Start at the beginning." Another beat. "Tell me everything."

Seth dragged a hand over his face. "It started a few weeks back. One day, a sandbag dropped. Not long after that, the grip truck was nearly set afire. Then, there was the day one of the dollies—the wheels were greased, brakes suddenly failed. Jimmy, one of our camera assistants, dove out of the way just in time. It was a miracle."

"Miracle, my eye," Clay snorted. "Somebody tampered with it. Cut the brake line clean through."

"Sounds deliberate."

"There's more." Clay turned to his brother. "Tell her."

Seth didn't want to. He clearly didn't want to. But it was too late to stop. "Gerry, one of our actors, got shocked by a prop lamp that'd been rigged with exposed wires. Nasty burn on his hand, could've been much worse."

"Don't forget the scaffold," Clay said. "How it collapsed last week. If it'd been a few minutes later, half the lighting crew would've been crushed."

I listened in growing concern as they recounted incident after incident. Someone had a vendetta against this film— and they didn't care who got hurt. Or perhaps that was the entire point.

An uneasy silence fell as the brothers finished their grim litany.

"Those aren't accidents," I said. "That's sabotage. Someone's deliberately trying to harm your production, putting people at risk."

"Show her the notes," Clay said.

But Seth was obviously reluctant to do so. He clenched his jaw, a muscle twitching beneath his smooth skin.

"Notes?" I prompted. "What notes?"

"Go on," Clay said. "You might as well."

"Yes," I echoed. "You might as well."

Seth's looked between his brother and me, then reluctantly reached down, yanked open a drawer and pulled out a stack of folded pages. Their edges were crumpled and worn, as though they'd been opened and closed many times.

"I've been receiving these. Threats, warnings … demands to stop filming. They coincided with the accidents on set."

He handed them to me and I unfolded the first one.

Shut it down, or suffer the consequences.

The second was no better.

We know every move you make. Every scene you shoot. Stop now, or pay the price.

Short but vicious. All variations of the same message. The language was cold, calculated and precise.

I looked up at Seth. "Who else knows about these?"

"Just us. I didn't want to panic the crew."

"Panic them?" Clay repeated. "They're putting their lives on the line every time they step onto that set. They deserve to know—if they don't suspect already."

"You need to find out who's behind this," I said. "Before someone gets seriously hurt ... or worse." I glanced at the notes again. "Whoever wrote these, he knows this set backwards and forwards."

"See?" Clay said, as if resuming an argument they'd had before. "She thinks someone on set is behind this, too."

Seth didn't answer right away. He stared at the floor, his hands braced on the edge of the desk. "I don't know. I don't want to believe it."

"You don't—you don't *want* to?" Clay was incredulous. "Open your eyes, brother! This isn't just bad luck. Someone's messing with us—and it's an inside job."

"I can't accept that." Seth turned to me. "Look, I *know* these people. They're like family. None of them would do this."

Clay shook his head. "Just because you feel that way doesn't mean they do. Family or not, someone's trying to sabotage this film."

I drew a deep breath. "Seth, I know this is difficult, but you have to consider all possibilities. Who has access to the set? Who knows the production well enough to be behind this?"

He shrugged, raising open palms. "Everyone. The actors. The whole crew. We've been working together for years, some of us since my very first film."

Clearly, he did not want to face the harsh but very likely possibility that someone he trusted had betrayed him. I glanced at the crumpled notes. Threats, sabotage, the accidents that weren't accidents at all but proof of a malevolent mind at work—it was all there. I studied Seth's face. Exhaustion and strain were aging him beyond his years.

"Have you told the police?" I glanced between the two of them. Their expressions gave me the answer. "You have to report this."

Clay let out another bitter snort, folding his arms across his chest. "The police won't care. You think they're gonna come running 'cause a colored man's film set is falling apart? They'd laugh us out of the station."

"Maybe," I said. "But you should at least try. Someone's out to get you. And they're taking no prisoners. The risk to you—and to everyone who works around you—it's just too high to ignore."

I paused for a beat, letting my words sink in. Then I looked directly at Seth. "And I have to write about it. The public has a right to know what's happening here."

Both of them stiffened at that. Clay gave a grunt, looked away and shook his head. Like he was done. Just done with the whole argument.

Seth's expression darkened. Sparks of panic flickered in his eyes. "Please. Give us a little time. Let us try to figure out who's behind this before it turns into a scandal. This film, it means everything to me—to us." His gesture took in Clay. "I can't let it fail because of this."

His eyes searched mine for something—empathy, maybe. Or mercy. "If word gets out about these accidents, about the sabotage ... it could ruin everything. The people who've invested money, those who've promised to? They'll pull out. And if they do, that's it. No more film. No more jobs. Maybe even no more career."

I understood what he was saying and I certainly sympathized, but I couldn't just look away. "People's lives are at risk. You can't just ignore that."

"I know, I know." He drew a deep breath, then let it out slowly. "Lanie ... *Miss* Lanie," he said, adding that Southern term of respect. "Please." He swallowed. "All I'm asking for is a little time. The picture's nearly done. We're so close." He raised a hand as if reaching for a goal, then tightened it into a fist as though he'd attained it. "Almost there."

I glanced at Clay, who looked just as tense, though his frustration was quieter, then turned back to Seth.

"And what about the next time?" I asked. "'Cause as sure as I'm standing here, there *will* be a next time. Whoever's behind this mess is playing for keeps. His eye is on the clock just as much as yours is. And he's not about to let it run out on whatever nasty game he's running."

Seth closed his eyes, twisted his neck—I could hear the muscles crack—then he set his shoulders. And I knew in that moment what he was going to say.

"I can figure this out. And I can stop him—or them—from doing any more damage. I have fought too hard, come too far, to let anyone get in my way." He paused, then pointed to the set beyond his office door. "You're right. Those people out there, they're depending on me. For jobs. For a way to feed their families. For a way to keep the damn lights on at night. And I'm not gonna fail them. Not today. And not tomorrow."

He leveled his gaze at me. "Now, I can't tell you how to do your job. But I can ask you—even beg you—to have a little faith in me. I will bring this ship into port. I'll do it fast. I'll do it smooth. With no lives lost—if you just give me—give *us*, my brother and me—the chance."

Two brothers, both of them, looking to me. It was as if the whole world had stopped, was just waiting on little old me to make my decision. And I suppose the whole world *had*—their world, anyway.

I hesitated, torn between my duty as a reporter and the raw plea in their eyes. I had a job to do. And people's safety hung in the balance. But then there was Seth—a man standing on the edge of something fragile, trying to hold his dream together while everything around him seemed to fall apart.

"I can't stay quiet forever." I said, surprised at the words coming out of my mouth. "So you'd better get this movie wrapped up or find out who's behind this—and fast. Because if someone else gets hurt, I won't be able to hold off."

Seth exhaled. He and his brother exchanged glances and a relieved nod.

"Not a victory," I said. "Just a temporary reprieve."

"I know." Seth chanced a relieved smile. "I'll figure it out. I promise."

I couldn't believe I had agreed and I'm pretty sure, neither could they. Now that I'd given my word, I had to wonder: How much longer could Seth hold everything together? And how long could I wait before I'd have to blow it all wide open?

4

Clay walked me back out, our footsteps echoing against the scuffed wooden floorboards. Black and white photographs lined the hallway along the way. Photos of actors, hopefuls? A couple I recognized, but the others? They didn't ring a bell. What had happened to them? As I walked by their portraits, I could almost hear them, whispering. Stories of forgotten dreams and lost ambitions. I thought of Seth and his fear that with one word I could destroy his film, his career—and put dozens of people out of work.

"I'm glad you were here today." Clay walked with his head down, thoughtful. "I'm sorry there was another incident, but I'm glad you were here to see it."

His words surprised me. "Why? Aren't you scared of me writing about it?"

"Oh, don't get me wrong. I am. If anything, I'm more worried about it than he is. No, what I meant was, it was good to have a set of outside eyes. My brother and I, we're too close. And he ... well, he tends to stick his head in the sand."

"Yes," I smiled, "he's a visionary."

"He's more than that. He's ... idealistic. Noble, even." He paused, came to a standstill and sighed. "But nobility don't pay the bills."

I noticed the deep creases etched into his forehead. "Is it that bad?"

"Worse than he lets on." Clay was thoughtful, then gave a little grunt. "Sometimes I wonder if my brother's dreams will be the death of us."

A particularly apt, if morbid, expression, in light of the dangerous sabotage plaguing the film set and Seth's determination to forge on. The saboteur would be to blame if harm came to anyone, but Seth's insistence on not saying anything meant that he'd also bear some of the responsibility.

The light from the lone bulb overhead threw Clay's features into sharp relief, deepened the shadows under his eyes.

"Seth's a dreamer," I said. "It's probably what draws people to him. That unwavering belief that anything is possible."

Clay sighed, shoved his hands deep into his pockets. "Belief alone can't hold up the walls forever. Sooner or later, the cracks show. And when they do ..." His voice trailed off as he stared down the empty corridor stretching before us.

I sensed his loyalty and his frustration. It seems that Seth's determined idealism was both his greatest strength and his fatal flaw. How long could he keep this precarious balancing act going before everything came crashing down around him?

"Seth seems to think he can figure out who's behind this. Does this mean that you two suspect someone?"

"Seth? No, he doesn't suspect anyone. You heard him. As far as he's concerned, everyone on this set can be trusted."

"But you don't feel that way."

"I'm ... well, I'm more of a realist. And yes, I do suspect someone." He paused. "Name of Westbrook—Sydney Westbrook."

"And he is ...?"

"Our main camera man." Clay nodded to himself. "Yeah. He's needs a good looking at. Look, Westie's good at his job —I know 'cause I sometimes help him out with the lighting . He's old school. Used to be Seth's mentor. But now he's fighting Seth at every turn. Just yesterday, he nearly punched Seth out over a damn setup."

"Really?" That information surprised me. I could under-stand Seth's impulse to protect his crew. But it was unset-tling to think he'd overlook the kind of conflict Clay was describing.

Clay gave a small grunt. "Watching them try to work together is like watching two storms collide."

"But they used to get on all right?"

"That was when Seth was young. It was before he started having his own ideas."

"So, the apprentice has now become the master."

"Exactly. Seth's trying to create something new and exciting, not just in terms of story—that's there for sure—he also wants to try out new camera angles. He's a stickler for the little things, too, like making sure the close-ups are done right, that every actor is seen in his or her best light—literally."

"I'd think Westbrook very capable of—"

"That's what Westbrook thinks, too. He doesn't like the idea of someone younger telling him what to do and how to do it. He's so stuck in his ways. Hangs on to them like a drowning man to a life raft. Can't see beyond his own ego."

Clay frowned. "As a matter-of-fact ..."His voice trailed away, as he paused.

"Yes?"

He glanced at me. "I was just thinking. The last blowup? It happened this morning. Seth had this grand vision for a scene, wanted to use these bold, experimental angles to capture the raw emotion of it. But Westbrook? He wouldn't have it. Had to stick to his tried-and-true. Said Seth's ideas were too risky, too untested."

I didn't know Sydney Westbrook, had never heard of him before, but I had an immediate mental picture of him. Gray-haired, cantankerous and tough, with skin like leather and more stubborn than a mule. I could also picture Seth, determined to make his picture his way, facing off against the older man's rigid resistance. That kind of confrontation could destroy morale and tear the very fabric of the film apart.

"It got ugly," Clay continued. "They went at it for hours, arguing over every little detail until the crew was ready to mutiny. Wasted all that time. Money counts in this business. Literally. Seth acts like he's worried about our budget but I'm the one counting every dime. And those dimes turn into dollars fast—lost dollars—when you have the two of them going at it like that."

I stopped to gaze up at Clay—he was at least a head taller than me. "You sound as though you blame Seth."

"I do—and I don't. He lets Westbrook get away with too much. That's all I'm saying. The man's a menace. Seth should've let him go a long time ago."

"Why doesn't he?"

Clay reflected a moment, then shrugged. "Loyalty, I

guess. There's no other way to explain it. You saw him back there. He talks about bringing ugly truths to the surface, but he can barely see the truth when it's right under his nose."

I felt some sympathy for Seth. But I also understood Clay's frustration. It wasn't enough to have a vision, you had to be practical, too. Otherwise, you were just building a house of cards. One hard gust of wind and it would all fall apart.

5

An hour later, I was back at the *Chronicle's* newsroom, amid the din of ringing phones and the clatter of typewriters. I glanced up at Sam's office. He was inside, working a stack of articles. I'd have to brief him about the sabotage. He would agree that it was important. And for that very reason, he'd want to print it immediately. How could I justify delaying it?

I took a deep breath and set my shoulders. The air held the lingering odor of ink and paper. It wasn't a scent that many people would find pleasant. But I did. It grounded me, reassured me. I drew strength from it, from its familiarity.

I slipped my purse into one of my side desk drawers. The July heat seeped through the open windows. Beads of perspiration formed along my hairline. I wiped them away with the back of my hand, then strode down the aisle between our desks to Sam's office.

His door was slightly ajar. Inside, shafts of afternoon sunlight slanted across his desk, illuminating stacks of manuscripts and a dead cup of coffee. A worn plaque sat on his desk, the letters faded, dust settled in its grooves. "Truth

First." He'd brought it with him when he joined the *Chronicle*.

He looked up as I entered. His eyes softened just a fraction when they met mine. Then his expression went from concentration on his work to curiosity and concern.

"You okay?" he asked.

"I'm fine, but yes, there is something I need to tell you."

I described the set—a labyrinth of creativity and chaos, now tainted by deliberate mishaps. Props misplaced, lights malfunctioning and scenes having to be reshot, risking lives and driving up costs. Each incident seemed minor alone, but together, they painted a sinister picture. Then there were the notes, which left no doubt.

"Sounds like a whale of story," Sam said. "How fast do you think you can get it to me?"

I stood there a moment, feeling uncomfortable. "That's the thing. When Mr. Carter confided in me, he asked for time to uncover whoever is behind this."

Sam leaned back in his chair, his brow furrowing deeper. "And what did you say?"

I felt like a child trying to explain herself to the school principal, a feeling I hated. Of course, I realized I had no one to blame but myself, but that didn't make me feel any better. If anything, it made me feel worse.

"I said I would think about it." I paused, realizing that wasn't quite accurate. "No, I said I would."

Sam raised his left eyebrow. "Did you now? And why's that?" He held his blue pencil by both ends, slowly turning it as he leveled his gaze at me.

"Well," I swallowed. "I agreed with him. That's why. I could see his point."

"About what?"

The faint hum of the newsroom faded, replaced by the

rhythmic pounding of my own pulse. I drew in a deep breath and began, choosing my words with care.

"If I—if *we*—report the story now, the result would be—it would end the film. Seth would have to shut it down. And that would be a huge loss, not just for him and those who work for him, with him, but for our community. I feel as though we'd be helping the saboteur accomplish his goals, when it's really Seth we need to support. We need to give Seth a chance to fix this."

Sam inclined his head. "Oh, is it '*Seth*' now?"

I started to answer, then thought better of it.

Sam's gaze stay on me. I could feel him mentally dissecting my argument with the precision of a scalpel. "But you yourself said that every ... 'mishap' endangers lives—"

"Yes, but those people, the people at risk, are aware of what's going on. They know the risk they're taking. And they're still willing to take it."

"Because they need the work."

"And because they believe in the film."

He slowly nodded. But that didn't mean he agreed. It simply meant he was taking in what I said, turning it over. His eyes grew distant, as he considered the matter.

Sam had given me a lot of leeway in the past, but this was pushing the limit—and I knew it. I found myself holding my breath. Outside, the July sun beat down hot and heavy against the window. Sam's office felt like an oven.

"Do you really want to sit on this?" he asked.

To be honest, I had my own doubts about the matter. I wasn't a classic "news hound" by any means, but I did consider myself a good reporter and I believed in the 'people's right to know." However, sometimes, that right had to be balanced with other considerations. "It's for the greater good."

He wagged his head from side to side. "Think about it," he said. "Think about what we're risking. Our readers count on us for the truth. Delaying this story could backfire and we might lose their trust."

"I understand, but if we expose the sabotage now, it will kill the project before they can fix it. The whole community's counting on this film. It's more than just a story; it's hope."

Sam's lips pressed into a straight line. His silence was more telling than words. I braced myself, anticipating his verdict. Finally, he gave a single nod, his decision made.

"Tell Seth Carter to get his ducks in a row—and fast. He's got a week to figure this out. That's it. In the meantime, you can write up today's interview."

I could barely believe my ears. "Not mentioning the sabotage."

He nodded. "Not mentioning the sabotage."

"Thank you." I didn't bother to hide my relief.

He laid his pencil aside. "Still on for dinner at my place tonight?"

"Wild horses couldn't keep me away." I allowed myself a small smile, the first since entering his office.

6

A warm summer breeze drifted in through the open window of Sam's modest kitchen and the sizzle of butter and herbs filled it, mingling with the rich scent of roasting chicken. I leaned against the counter, watching him chop carrots with surgical precision. The rhythmic tap-tap of his knife against the cutting board felt almost hypnotic.

"Come on, Lanie," he teased, "You can at least chop these vegetables." His eyes held a playful glint. He knew I couldn't cook worth a lick and felt totally lost in a kitchen.

"Chop?" I eyed the carrots with suspicion.

"Like this." His swift motions produced perfect, uniform squares. He slid over a small cutting board and held out the knife, handle first. My fingers fumbled over the smooth surface. The handle felt clumsy in my grip. I tried to mimic him, but the result was a massacre of uneven chunks.

"More abstract art than culinary skill." He grinned and I couldn't help but laugh.

I thought my performance with the carrots would save me from further kitchen duty. But I was wrong. Sam wasn't ready to give up.

"It's just a matter of practice." He handed me a bulb of garlic and another small knife. "I promise it won't bite."

"Sure about that?" I viewed the garlic with wary eyes, seeing it for what it was—a squat little adversary that was out to get me.

"Go on," he said, watching me. "Peel and mince."

"Peel and mince," I repeated under my breath. I put the knife to the garlic and went to work. The peeling part went fine, but then it came to the mincing. Bits of garlic flew everywhere. One clove skittered across the floor. It landed at Sam's feet like it was begging him for protection.

Sam chuckled, scooped it up and rinsed it off. "At this rate, we won't be eating till next week."

"Well, Sam, you know me and the kitchen don't get along."

"You're doing fine." He came up behind me, placed the clove on my cutting board, put his arms around me and guided my hands to show me the right technique. His touch sent an electric current down my spine.

But the garlic refused to cooperate. It slipped from my fingers. I threw my hands up, exasperated. "I give up."

"Not so fast." He scooped up the remaining mangled cloves and tossed them into the pan. "You can't escape that easily."

"Watch me." I stepped back, crossing my arms.

"Fine, you're off kitchen duty." He raised his hands in surrender. "But you can still make yourself useful and pour us some wine."

"Now *that* I can do."

I moved to the table he'd set earlier. Candles flickered softly, casting shadows that danced across the room. Sam opened a secret panel on the sideboard and produced a bottle of rosé. Contraband. Sam didn't say how he got it and

I didn't ask—some things are better left unsaid. The French label suggested it had been slipped past the feds, smuggled in from overseas. Sam must've paid a pretty penny for it. He handled it with reverence, like a rare treasure.

I uncorked it, enjoying its delicate aroma, then poured two glassfuls. The pale pink liquid shimmered in the candlelight.

"To survival in the kitchen." I raised my glass toward him.

"To survival. Period." He winked, his eyes catching the candlelight.

We clinked glasses and, for a moment, the world seemed to recede. For a moment, it was just the two of us.

He went back to cooking and I went back to doing what I do best—observing. I leaned against the counter, sipping wine and took note of his every move. From the joy in his face to the rippling muscles under his shirt to the toned belly, narrow hips and strong legs. He was handsome, yes. But it was more than that. There was a serenity in his movements—a man in his element, creating something beautiful out of simple ingredients. I felt intensely grateful to know him, to be there, to be the subject of his kindness, his affections.

Yet, I felt as though a glass wall stood between us, as though I were inside a cage that would forever set me apart. Funny that. As a child, I'd wondered if I'd always be the outsider looking in. Now, I was the insider, looking out. And I'd found, as any prisoner will tell you, that being walled in is just as unpleasant as being walled out.

The aroma of herb-roasted chicken filled his kitchen. I closed my eyes, inhaled deeply. The rich, savory smells of sage and thyme were comforting. They eased tension I didn't realize I'd been holding.

And just like that, thoughts of Hamp came to me, memories of times when he'd cook and I'd keep him company, swapping jokes, his laughter echoing through our home.

"Ready?"

Sam's voice brought me back. He'd plated the food and now led me to his table. He'd set it with a quiet elegance—white linen napkins, gleaming silverware, romantic candlelight. He started to sit, then thought better of it and stepped out. A second later, the dusky strains of the Duke's *"East St. Louis Toodle-Oo"* slid out of the living room gramophone. The muted growl of the trumpet was seductive and bittersweet. I'd always loved that low, slinking rhythm. But it was known for putting ideas—naughty ideas—in a respectable mind. And the fact that he had it on ... Well, that said something, didn't it?

We sat down and I couldn't help but notice how the light softened his features. He looked ... vulnerable. His usual sharp wit and directness seemed tempered and for a brief moment, I saw the raw tenderness he tried to hide.

I took a sip of wine, letting its crisp, dry notes linger on my tongue. The faintest hint of summer berries and citrus paired perfectly with the meal before us.

We began to eat and each bite was a revelation. The chicken was succulent, the creamy mashed potatoes a perfect comfort. The vegetables were crisp yet yielding and with subtlety spiced. The meal spoke of care, of love, of a man who wanted to nourish not just my body but my soul.

But there was an undercurrent I couldn't ignore. I brushed my fingertips against the stem of my wine glass, felt the cool, smooth surface. The music, the food, the setting—it all felt carefully staged.

"How is it?"

"Perfect." The word felt inadequate. It wasn't just the food that was perfect—it was the effort, the thoughtfulness behind it. I heard a little voice say, *Perfection has its price, doesn't it?*

He leaned back, studying me. That penetrating gaze. It had always made me feel seen, truly seen and I'd welcomed that feeling. But that evening, it made me squirm.

The shadows of the candlelight danced on the walls, twisting, sinuous, bewitching in their own way. The music played on, alluring, inviting. With each passing second, the atmosphere grew more intimate.

It felt both safe and terrifying.

The meal ended, but the lingering aroma of roasted garlic and thyme mixed with the smoky undertones of seared meat still filled the air. The soft glow from the candles cast a warm light across Sam's face, highlighting the concern etched into his features. I traced the lines of his jaw, the curve of his lips. I wanted him, wanted to be with him, build something with him, but ...

A knot tightened in my chest, a familiar ache that refused to be ignored. It wasn't that I didn't love him. God knows I did. But every glance, every touch, seemed to pull me deeper into a future I couldn't fully embrace. Hamp's ghost lingered in the corners of my mind, whispering reminders of promises unkept and dreams unfulfilled.

Sam's hand found mine again across the table. His fingers were warm and reassuring. I squeezed back, forcing a smile, but my heart wasn't in it. The jazz playing softly in the background only amplified the sense of longing for what I'd lost. Each note evoked memories I couldn't forget.

As we finished, he got up, moving with a purpose that made my pulse quicken. From behind him, he produced a small box I hadn't noticed before. It was elegantly wrapped in deep blue paper and tied with a silver ribbon. He placed it in front of me.

It filled my vision.

Anticipation mingled with dread. The box was beautiful, almost too perfect to disturb. Its crisp edges and meticulous folds suggested care and thought. Was this really what I feared it was? A ring? An invitation to step forward, to leave the past behind.

If so, then it was too soon. *Way too soon.*

I hesitated, reached for it, then drew back. The room seemed to contract and the walls pressed in. I could feel Sam's eyes on me, searching for a sign.

Opening the box would mean crossing a line. It would mean accepting a future that I wasn't ready to consider.

I looked up at Sam and in his eyes, I saw not just love but an earnest plea. He wanted this, wanted us, to move beyond the shadows that clouded our path. But could I?

The box sat between us, a sign of where we were and where we could go. I took a deep breath, then picked it up.

The cool, smooth ribbon beneath my fingers. I could feel Sam's gaze, sense him holding his breath.

The box opened with a soft click. A single, gleaming item lay nestled in deep blue velvet.

Not an engagement ring, but a key.

The key to Sam's apartment.

The key to his heart.

"Come and go as you please. My place is your place."

Nice words. Meant to ease my nerves. But they only made things worse. Sam's was putting his heart on the line. He wanted me to make his place my own, to share more than just evenings and laughter. My fingers brushed against the cold metal and I felt both the promise and the pressure it carried.

I should've been happy. But I couldn't be. One question ricocheted through my mind: Was I supposed to reciprocate with a key of my own?

How could I? That house wasn't just bricks and mortar; every inch carried memories of Hamp, of the dreams that died when he did, gone from a heart attack at thirty-three.

I picked up the key from its velvet bed and glanced at Sam. His hopeful eyes searched mine for a sign, any indication that I was ready to take this leap. But my heart clenched at the very idea.

The candlelight glinted off the polished wood of the table. My fingertips traced the smooth surface of the box, feeling the ridges of the ribbon. Words formed and dissolved before they could be voiced.

How could I explain to Sam that it wasn't about him, but the ghosts that still haunted me? I couldn't envision anyone but Hamp holding a key to that townhouse, wandering its rooms, filling them with the life we'd planned but never lived. Giving someone else that key felt like a betrayal.

"Sam, this is ... a big step."

His expression shifted—hurt visible for a split second before he shut it down. "I understand. No pressure. I just thought... well, I thought it was time."

"It's not ... you. It's just ... Well, I'm not sure I'm ready." I placed the key back in the box and closing the lid. The soft click felt like a door being shut between us.

He just nodded pensively. His fingers closed around the box slowly, almost reluctantly, as if taking it back physically pained him. Then, a question: "Not ready now. Will you ever be?"

My heart thumped. It was fair, the question, but what could I say?

Nothing adequate. That's for sure.

"Thank you. For the dinner. It ... it was wonderful." I stood, pushed back my chair, my movements stiff. The scrape of wood against wood was loud in the awkward silence.

I hurried down the hall to his living room and grabbed my purse, then headed to his front door. I needed to get out, get away. To breathe. To think.

"Lanie?" I heard his voice behind me, felt his presence.

I paused, one hand on the doorknob, my back to him. "I'm sorry," I whispered, then went out. I knew that I'd hurt him and that I may have made a mistake but I couldn't how I felt.

I stepped into the hallway and started down the stairs. Each step was heavier than the last. Behind me, through the door I'd just closed, I heard the sound of something soft hitting the wall. Then silence.

I hesitated.

What was I doing? Leaving like this. Turning him down. What—

I turned and started back up. Then froze, hands gripping the banister.

What good would going back do? My feelings hadn't changed. And what could I say? That I was trapped in a house of memories I couldn't escape? That I wasn't rejecting him, just unable to move forward? The words stayed locked in my throat.

I had made my decision, right or wrong.

My hands trembled on the banister as I made my way down and my knees threatened to buckle. Each step felt like walking through molasses. At some point, my vision blurred. I wiped my eyes with the back of my hands and held my head up high. Down the stairs I went, trying hard not to think about keys and homes and the good men who offer them.

Outside, the humid summer night met me with a rush of fetid air. And the sounds of city crashed over me—voices from stoops and fire escapes, a radio playing through an open window, children's laughter from a late game of stick-ball, the murmur of couples walking arm in arm. Life was rushing past at full throttle while I stood still.

I glanced up and caught a glimpse of Sam silhouetted in the window. The sight tugged at me, at an ache I couldn't ease. I turned away and moved deeper into the darkness, leaving behind the intimacy of Sam's kitchen, the promise of his key and the man who wanted to build a bridge across the chasm of my grief.

7

W e'd fallen in love with the townhouse at first sight —and used to joke it had fallen for us, too. From the moment Hamp and I stepped foot in it, it had made us feel welcome. Empty, unfurnished, it felt like it had been waiting for us. Like it already knew our names

It sat on the south side of West 139th Street, between Seventh and Sixth Avenues. Limestone. I'd only seen limestone on courthouses or banks, never a home. But there it was—clean and elegant, simple and refined. It was a gloomy February morning, gloomy and wet. But even under slate gray skies, the house managed to glow.

Then there was the neighborhood. Good people. Professionals. People who kept to themselves. Seventh Avenue could be as loud as a circus. But on Strivers' Row, it was still. (Hamp used to say it was so quiet, you could not only hear your own thoughts, but other people's, too.)

Now, walking back from Sam's place, the house rose ahead, its pale stone catching the orange wash of the streetlamps. Steady and solid. A shelter through the worst of it. A sanctuary that had seen me through the worst nights of my life. The embodiment of everything I'd lost and everything I wasn't ready to share. Not even with Sam.

My hand rested on the iron banister.

"Remember when we first saw this place?" I murmured. "You were so excited. You lit up like a kid's on Christmas morning."

I could see it clear as yesterday—Hamp laughing, calling out from room to room, already making plans. Our voices echoing in that hollow space, building a life that hadn't happened yet.

Twelve rooms. Including three bedrooms—four, if we were organized. We were going to fill it with love. With laughter. With family.

That never happened. But it wasn't the house's fault. Sometimes I felt that it grieved with me. For Hamp. For the future we didn't get to finish.

I climbed the stairs, slid the key in the lock and stepped inside with a sense of relief. The scent hit me first—lemon polish and old wood. I shut the door and leaned against it. Safe. This house was the only place that felt like mine. It held my grief like a secret. Kept me company when I didn't want any.

But tonight, something felt different. As if the quiet wasn't comfort—it was a chain.

I set down my purse, kicked off my shoes and wandered into the parlor. So many memories were born here. The Chesterfield sofa where Hamp would sit, his medical journals spread around him. The mahogany sideboard that had held champagne flutes the day we toasted to our future here. Every detail whispered of him, of us.

I crossed the room, my heels soft against the hardwood. My fingers skimmed the back of the sofa. The leather smooth and cool beneath my touch. I'd picked it out just for him. Said it 'looked like a doctor's sofa.' He'd laughed and asked me what a doctor's sofa looked like.

I don't know. But this is it.

Yeah, he'd laughed. I guess it is.

And it had been. For a while there, it had been.

Back to the hallway. Up the stairs. Each step an echo. At the top, the bedroom door stood open just enough to let the moon in. I pushed it wider.

The room was dim. Moonlight edged the silver frame on the nightstand. Hamp's photo. Grinning like he had all the time in the world.

I picked it up. Traced the line of his jaw, the curve of his smile.

"Oh, baby." I sat on the bed. "What happened to us?"

The day we got the keys. That was something. It was sunny that day. Bright and beautiful. Hamp walking through each room, his voice alive with plans. *"Just imagine, hon, what we can do here."*

I'd imagined it. A nursery, yellow walls. A little crib by the window. A shelf of stuffed animals waiting for arms that never came.

Names whispered in the dark—Emily if it was a girl. Marcus if it was a boy.

All of it gone the day Hamp collapsed in the street and never got up.

I remembered that morning. Rushing to meet a deadline, brushing past him in the hall. He'd wanted to talk —"Lanie, there's something I ought to tell you..."—but I'd waved him off with a quick kiss and an even quicker goodbye.

"Hold that thought. I'm late."

What had he wanted to tell me? I would never know for sure.

The next time I saw him, he was under a sheet at the city morgue.

No kiss. No goodbye. No second chances.

I set the photograph back down. Let my fingers rest against the glass.

Whatever he'd meant to say that morning—it died with him.

And I hadn't listened.

I stood and crossed to the wardrobe. Pulled out a clean blouse, set it on the chair. Tomorrow would come, same as always. And I'd be ready.

In the bathroom, I splashed cold water on my face, patted it dry. The woman in the mirror looked older than I remembered. Not tired—just worn at the edges.

I switched off the light, crossed the bedroom and drew the curtains shut.

Then I changed into my nightclothes, climbed into bed and lay still, listening to the silence. The kind Hamp used to say could carry more than your own thoughts.

8

I stopped by the set the next day to talk to Westbrook and found him in a makeshift office, lit by a bare bulb dangling from the ceiling. The place smelled of stale coffee and cigarette smoke. The walls were lined with heavy wooden shelves bearing cameras and parts of camera equipment. A rickety wood desk held stacks of lighting diagrams, shooting plans and drafts of scripts.

Despite this crowding, there was a strong sense of order. The cameras and their accessories were lined up like soldiers awaiting assignment. The corners of lighting diagrams, shooting plans and scripts on his desk were perfectly aligned.

Westbrook was hunched over a small lamp. It had delicate little crystals hanging from a satin shade. His broad fingers moved with surprising precision as he adjusted the metal clasp of one of the crystals with a pair of pliers.

"Mr. Westbrook?"

He straightened up. "Who's asking?" The cameraman wasn't all that tall, but he was broad-shouldered, strong and square. Reminded me of a stone wall. He was the one who'd muttered, "Third one this month."

"Lanie Price. I'm looking into the recent incidents on set."

He looked surprised. "Private detective?"

"No," I smiled faintly. "Reporter."

That response garnered even more surprise. "You mean, he's agreed to talk to the press?"

"I was on-set yesterday when the rigging fell. He didn't have much choice."

"Oh, yeah, I remember." He turned back to the lamp. "So, what do you want from me?"

I leaned against the rickety table, feeling the rough wood against my hips. "These incidents. You have to admit, they look suspicious. And you've made no secret of your issues with Seth."

"Ah." He gave a grunt. "You think I'm behind it all?"

"Your disagreements have been compared to watching two storms collide."

He almost smiled at that one. "Creative differences? Sure. We've had a few. But sabotage? That's absurd." He straightened. "Look, I may not like the way Seth runs every scene, but I'd never hurt this film. It means too much to me —to all of us."

"You have the knowledge to—"

"So do a lot of people. What's been going on here, it don't take much. Loosen a screw here, a screw there and you got it. A spotlight falls. A little bit of know-how—and a whole lot of malice. That's all it takes. Just about anybody who works here could be doing it."

Maybe, that was true. Maybe, it wasn't. Either way, he was missing one key fact: "But not everyone's had your recent clashes with him."

Westbrook's dark eyes flashed with frustration. "I won't deny the arguments. Seth and I? We've locked horns more times than I can count. He's got a whole lot of big ideas— but he doesn't have the time, the money, or the equipment to back them up. And that has led to trouble."

The weak light from the single bulb overhead threw deep shadows across his features. It made it hard to read his expression. But I didn't have to. His voice told me all I needed to know. The old man wasn't just frustrated. He felt insulted. I could understand that. I didn't enjoy making people feel insulted. But it came with the territory. You ask enough questions and it happens. So his hurt feelings didn't bother me. What bothered me was that he made sense.

A lot of sense.

"But," he went on, "I respect what he's trying to do. Always have. I've seen him grow from a kid full of ideas to someone who can make them land. I'd never do anything to block his success or the success of this movie."

Thunder rumbled through the walls, barely audible over the set noise outside.

"Here, let me show you something." Westbrook put down the pliers and went to the desk. Reached up to a shelf above the desk, took down a framed photograph and handed it to me. The image must've been at least fifteen years old. It showed a younger Westbrook standing beside a beaming Seth. Their arms were slung around each other's shoulders and they were holding an award between them.

Westbrook tapped the picture. "Seth and I, we go back a long way. This picture was taken when Seth first got out of school. I was a teacher back then, not full-time, just part-time for the fun of it."

"And he was one of your students?"

"That little award there, it was just something I rigged up for him. The boy had talent. Still does."

I handed him back the photo. He carefully put it back in place. Then he turned back to me. "Let me ask you something. Who put you on to me? Clay?"

My silence answered him.

"Thought so." He stepped closer, his broad frame looming over me. Then he reached past me, pulled open a drawer, the metal handle squeaking as he tugged it open. After a moment of rummaging, he pulled out a folded piece of paper. Its edges were softened with handling.

"I didn't have a lot to give, but I gave what I had and I don't want to lose it." Westbrook's fingers trembled slightly as he unfolded the document and handed it to me.

It was a financial agreement that detailed Westbrook's investment in the film. The sum was modest by a rich man's reckoning, but significant for an old cameraman. The document was signed and notarized, a tangible proof of his stake in the project.

"Listen, I've been here since day one. Put my money where my mouth is. You think I'd sabotage my own investment?"

I ran my fingers over the embossed seal. The rough texture confirmed its authenticity.

He let out a sad laugh. "Seth's always been a dreamer. That's not news. And yes, we argue. But we argue because we both care about the picture. He wants to push boundaries. I want to make sure we get it done. You can call it a clash of egos if you want, but it's not sabotage."

"What would you call it, then?"

"Reality."

Outside, there was a burst of thunder and the summer rain began to fall. The steady patter of raindrops beat against the roof. The damp air seeped through the cracks in the walls.

I looked up at Westbrook, seeing him in a new light. The determination in his eyes matched the money he'd put down. I carefully folded the document and handed it back to him. "But if not you, then who?"

Westbrook's gaze went to the small window,. Rain shadows played across his face. "Grace. Seth's wife."

"Grace?" I frowned. "But she—why would she—?"

"She has dreams of her own."

I have to admit I was dumbfounded. I started to ask another question, but he raised a finger to his lips. "And that's all I'm saying."

9

The heat radiated off the pavement in shimmering waves as I arrived at the Little Harlem Theater, a small vaudeville venue on East 125th Street. The marquee proclaimed "Coming Soon: Grace Carter's Visionary Production."

Inside, Grace stood center stage, directing a trio of actors through a complex scene. Her presence filled the theater.

"Hold that pose."

She had the effortless poise of someone who has mastered both sides of the spotlight. Moving to a young actress, she showed her the angle she needed. The girl followed the cue perfectly and Grace nodded in approval.

"There. Now you're capturing the moment instead of chasing it."

Grace spotted me at the back of the theater and called for a break. "Five minutes, everyone."

She beckoned me to the side steps. The other actors watched her go with both respect and envy. Even in a simple day dress, she had the presence of someone standing center stage.

"Lanie. I wondered when you'd come calling."

Her ruby ring caught the light as we shook hands.

"Grace. Thank you for seeing me."

"I assume this isn't a social call."

Backstage was busy with the excited chatter of stage-hands checking equipment and actors running lines. The scent of fresh paint and sawdust tickled my nose. She led me into a small office. Posters of past productions adorned its walls. Blueprints were spread out on a side table. She closed the door behind us with a soft click.

"Something to drink? Coffee?"

"No, thank you. I'm fine."

She settled behind her desk with the same fluid motion I'd seen on stage. She took out a cigarette case and offered me one. I declined and sat opposite.

"So," I began. "Seth's film has problems."

"Yes, well, problems do have a way of finding ambitious projects, don't they?" She reached for the silver lighter on her desk.

"Several accidents in a month isn't just bad luck."

Grace struck the lighter. The flame caught, its reflection dancing in her dark eyes as she lit her cigarette. "That set's been under pressure. Tempers flare. Not everyone adapts well to the new pace Seth demands. Especially those who've been around a long time." She inhaled deeply, then clicked the lighter shut and set it down. "What exactly do you need from me?"

"Someone's sabotaging the film. Someone with access, knowledge and motive. I'm trying to understand who benefits if *Soul Redemption* fails."

"Are you? Or are you just digging for dirt?" She smiled to take some of the sting out—some, not all. "We've built something here. Carter Films isn't just Seth and me. It's a family. And families don't always take well to outsiders sniffing around."

Holding her cigarette high, she blew a stream of smoke into the air. "Now, Seth told me you'd agreed not to mention what happened yesterday or last week. Yet, here you are."

"I promised I wouldn't write anything—right now. But I still need to understand what's happening."

She studied me, smoke veiling her face like lace. "You'll forgive me for being so direct, but I've been burned by reporters before—especially by ones I like and who I thought liked me."

"You needn't worry—"

"But I do. Seth's a big boy. He should know how to protect himself. But he doesn't. Not always."

"And so it falls to *you* ..."

"Exactly." She took another drag of her cigarette, tapped it over the ashtray. "If you think I'd sabotage Seth's film, you're wasting your time. And mine. I have my own dreams, my own ambitions, yes. But sabotage Seth's work? Never. That would be cutting my own throat."

She made it easy to believe her—as charming as any diva.

"Why would you even think I'd suspect you?"

She laughed. "Because you're here. You're a reporter. And right now, you're weighing my words like you're pricing diamonds on credit."

"It's my job to question."

"And mine to convince." She was silent a moment, thinking. "How about this? I'm a woman of the theater, the stage. I can direct an actor from twenty feet away, but a camera dolly? A lighting rig?" She gave a dismissive gesture. "They might as well be machinery from the moon."

That could be true. Theater and film were different worlds, each with its own language, its own equipment.

However, the two worlds weren't mutually exclusive. Actors crossed the boundaries, worked in both mediums, all the time. And they gained knowledge about both.

Of course, Grace could've been one of those performers who had absolutely no interest in learning the technical aspects of filmmaking, who resisted it, in fact. But there was a simple solution to that.

"You wouldn't need to know how. Just who to ask."

"An accomplice." She inclined her head thoughtfully and gave a little nod. "Smart angle. Except ..."

She picked up her ashtray and walked to the table with the blueprints.

"Maybe, I should mention, this will be my last picture with Seth."

"Really? Why?"

"There's no trouble in paradise, if that's what you're thinking. Quite the opposite."

She bid me to come stand beside her. "You and I, we both know that dreams aren't just pretty things you hang on the wall. They've got teeth."

She spread out the large sheets.

"I've spent ten years playing other people's stories when I could've been creating my own. I've earned my freedom. Now, it's my turn."

She gestured to the theater plans with a sweep of her hand, ash barely clinging to her cigarette. "This theater, these renovations—they're mine. When the film wraps, I'm launching my own company."

"Sounds like you're eager to move on."

"I've put everything into each frame of Seth's films. But the stage has always been where I truly breathe."

"And Seth ...?"

She tapped her cigarette over the ashtray with precise movements. "He and I understand each other. We're partners. The film does well, he helps fund this place. That's the deal. I finally get to create something that's mine. Not asking permission, not playing someone else's vision."

"You sound bitter."

"Do I? I'm just tired. I love my husband and I love what we've created together. But it's time to move on."

"So you wouldn't risk the one thing that gets you everything."

"Exactly."

"Then who would? Who benefits if the film fails?"

She took her time answering. "Everyone Seth ever fired. Anyone who didn't get the part. Or the credit. You want ten names? Twenty?"

She paused. "Wait. Let me ask you something. Why did you come see me today? Did Westie send you?"

"I told you. I—"

"Did he sic you on me? Give you some nonsense about me wanting to destroy my own husband's film?"

I gave her a half-smile. "I'm not a dog, Grace. No one 'sics' me on anything. I did have questions for you, yes."

She smiled cynically. "My, you are discrete, aren't you?"

"I try to be."

"Well, I hate to tell you, but Westie's not the man he used to be."

"You think he's behind this?"

She hesitated. "I've worked with him for years. But lately? His setups take longer. He second-guesses. And when Seth suggests something bold, something modern, *anything* that requires precision—he refuses. And then he accuses Seth of being difficult."

She leaned in close and lowered her voice confidentially. "Two weeks ago, Seth suggested a complicated tracking shot. Westie exploded, said it couldn't be done. Clay stepped in, worked out how to do it. You should have seen Westie's face."

"That doesn't make him a saboteur."

"No? But pride's a dangerous thing. What happens when a man knows he's slipping? Realizes he's losing everything that defines him?"

"Any proof?"

"Just what I see. And what Clay sees. He's been covering for Westie. Ask him."

She ground out the cigarette. "You came here thinking I was your saboteur. But ask yourself—what do I gain from ruining *Soul Redemption*? And what does Westie gain from proving he's still indispensable?"

I picked up my purse. "You make a compelling case. Then again, you're an actress. That's what actresses do." I smiled to take some of the sting out—some, not all.

But she didn't flinch. "Not this time. Seth's film matters too much—to both of us. We can't afford to let anyone tear it down."

"I'll look into Westbrook some more."

"Do that." She stood in the doorway, one hand on the frame. "When this is all over and Seth's film premieres, I hope you'll write about what he's accomplished rather than what almost stopped him."

She extended her hand again and clasped my hand with confident ease. "I believe in my husband's work. It matters too much—to all of us—to let anyone stand in its way."

I stepped into the hallway. The sounds of backstage preparations flooded back. Her words followed me.

What did I know for certain?

That someone wanted this film to fail.

And that nearly everyone had a reason to see it succeed.

Nearly everyone.

10

_____

I had a lot of ladies club meetings to attend after leaving Grace—meetings that were, believe it or not, part of my job. So it was near the end of the workday when I finally got to the newsroom.

Trouble was waiting. Typewriters stopped. Chairs creaked. Eyes turned away.

Sam called from his office. "Lanie. In here. *Now*."

As soon as I stepped inside, he thrust a newspaper at me. Didn't meet my eyes. Didn't say a word. When our fingers brushed, he pulled his hand quickly as if burned. It wasn't just anger I sensed, but something worse—resignation, plain and final.

I don't know if he was thinking about the key. I know I was—until I saw the paper, saw the headline.

The bold letters jumped off the page.

A FILM SET TO DIE FOR: THE
TROUBLED MAKING OF *SOUL REDEMPTION*

My stomach turned over.

Is Seth Carter's highly anticipated Soul Redemption doomed from the start? Unexplained accidents, financial woes and rumors of sabotage have cast a shadow over Mr. Carter's ambitious production. Sources close to the set describe mounting tensions and a director whose vision might be too grand for reality to handle. The production is reportedly spiraling out of control, plagued by mysterious accidents, fractured relationships and a mounting sense of dread.

"It's a disaster," said one source close to the production. "Every time we think we're back on track, something else goes wrong. It's like the film is cursed."

Some crew members are whispering that someone might be pulling strings behind the scenes to ensure Mr. Carter's failure. Others suggest the chaos is internal, a result of rising tensions among the cast and crew.

"People are scared," said another source. "One minute, it's a piece of equipment malfunctioning; the next, it's a set collapsing. No one feels safe. And the worst part is, we don't know who or what's behind it."

Some are pointing the finger at Mr. Carter himself, claiming his perfectionism is creating a toxic environment. "He demands everything, gives nothing and blames everyone else when things fall apart," said one disgruntled crew member.

While Mr. Carter remains tight-lipped, refusing to address the growing speculation, one thing is clear: Soul Redemption is teetering on the edge. With rising costs, a fractured crew and whispers of sabotage, the film's future is as uncertain as its troubled present.

The story was riddled with speculation and unnamed

sources. It was also effective. And very damaging. "How did they—?"

"Doesn't matter how. It's out there now." Sam tapped the byline. "Did you notice?"

I'd been so struck by the headline, I hadn't noticed the name of the reporter beneath it. Now I did.

Selena Troy.

I looked up. Sam pushed away from his desk, paced to the window. "Yeah. *Her.*"

Selena Troy. The ambitious little obit writer who'd moved through our newsroom like a rumor with a deadline—fast, corrosive and never burdened by facts. I hadn't thought of her in more than a year—not since she stormed out of the *Chronicle*, chasing dreams she swore were too big for our paper to handle.

I tossed the paper onto his desk. "She hasn't changed."

"Apparently not." Sam stayed at the window. A cloud passed over the sun, throwing shadows across his face. "She's still treating the news like it's her personal playground."

He went back to his desk, picked up the paper again and studied it like he still couldn't believe his eyes. "And now I've got to explain why one of my best reporters sat on a story while a death notice diva scooped us."

I sank into the chair across from his. "We're in trouble, aren't we?"

"Trouble doesn't begin to cover it. Management's demanding to know how we got scooped by this trash." He dropped the paper, rubbed his temples. "And the fact that it's her? That just makes it worse. Makes it look like we trained her up just to watch her bite us."

"She always wanted my column."

"Doesn't matter what she wants," Sam snapped. "What

matters is that she's dragging us into a mess we might not get out of. Management's furious and they have a right to be."

His office was hotter than ever, but I felt a chill. "The story isn't even accurate—"

"It's out there. That's what matters." He dropped down heavily in his chair. "It might be one of the worst pieces of reporting I've seen. But when it comes to the basic facts, it's telling the truth."

Sam rubbed his chin. "Management wanted to know if we knew about the sabotage. They knew you'd been there. I had to admit that yes, we knew. Claiming ignorance would've made us both look like fools."

The walls seemed to close in. The smell of ink and paper, usually comforting, now felt suffocating.

"But once I confirmed that," he went on, "I had to explain why we sat on it."

"Sam, I—"

"As you might guess, that did not go down well. Management wants the story. We put out something now or watch our reputation take a hit."

"But, Sam—"

"No ifs ands or buts about it. Your reason for staying silent is now moot."

"But—"

"Lanie, think. Holding back now will hurt Carter more than help him. At least, if you write it, you'll write it straight. Readers will get the facts, not this wild gossip—which, unsourced or not—hews closer to the truth than you'd like to admit."

Sam was right. But it still felt wrong to break a promise.

"You don't have a choice." Sam stood. "If you don't write the story, I'll make sure someone else does."

"But—"

He sliced the air with one hand. "This is bigger than a promise—especially one that never should've been made."

I wanted to argue but his expression stopped me cold. Beyond the office, typewriters clacked. Phones rang. The newsroom churned on while my world tilted sideways.

"Management wants the story and they want it now," Sam said. "But I was able to buy us some time."

"How much?"

"Two hours."

"Two hours?! But that's—"

"There's no room for negotiation. They didn't even want to give us that."

The only thing I could hear was the pounding of blood in my veins—and the ticking of Sam's clock on the wall.

"Look, Lanie, I know you wanted to help these people, but the time for that is long gone. And it's not just about the story anymore; it's about our credibility. We're the leading colored newspaper in New York City—the black *New York Times*—and we let ourselves get scooped by a scandal sheet."

His words hit home. I knew what he was asking, what he needed. He had taken the heat, defended me. I owed him.

"All right." I nodded. "Fine."

"Good." The tension in his shoulders eased. "Now get to work—and take this piece of trash with you."

I accepted the paper and got up to leave, but paused at the door. I don't know why. Maybe it was to apologize. But I wouldn't have known what I was apologizing for—whether it was for the key or the story.

He looked up at me. "Yes?"

I shook my head, "Nothing," and stepped out. His door slam shut behind me with a finality that made me flinch.

11

The newsroom was nearly empty now. Only a few desks remained lit. I hurried back to my desk, dropped Selena's paper on it and stood there, hands on my hips, staring at the byline.

Selena Troy.

The very name made me grit my teeth.

The phone rang. I knew who it was. "Seth? Hi. Let me expl—"

"Explain? What's to explain?" His voice was tight with anger. "You broke your promise. Now my investors are rushing for the exit door."

"Please. Listen. The story appeared in another newspaper, not mine. I have no control over what someone else prints. If I wanted the story out there, I would've written it myself, not leaked it to another paper—especially not a yellow rag like that. Someone else is behind this, maybe the same person or people who are sabotaging your set."

A pause. I could almost hear the gears in his mind turning.

"This is bad, Lanie, really bad. It's a mess. I don't even know where to begin to clean it up."

"You can start by seriously thinking about who could be behind this—or taking this to the police. As for me, I'm going to write the piece I should've written to begin with. Tells the facts. Calm, clear and reasonable."

"But won't that add fuel to the fire? Maybe, if we ignore it, don't add oxygen, it'll—"

"No, we've got to move on this. Control the fire. Control the narrative. If we don't, then we're conceding it to someone else, someone who doesn't give a damn about you, your film or the community-at-large."

He went quiet, turning the problem over, looking for a way out.

"Okay, okay. Do what you have to do." He sighed. "I can't stop you now, anyway, can I?"

"No. You can't."

We disconnected. I took a deep breath, massaged my temples and wondered where I could pilfer some headache medicine. Only a few lights left on. Rows of empty desks stretched out like a haunted library. Theoretically, lots of easy pickings.

Instead, I dropped down in my chair, leaned on my desk and buried my face in my hands. I had those club meetings to write up—excruciatingly boring stuff, but keeping a record of those meetings was important, at least to those who took part in them. Seeing their names in print? That told those ladies they'd made it, that what they were doing —teaching, organizing charities, funding nursing services— was known and acknowledged. Had made it into the record.

Furthermore, that kind of news was my bread and butter —and it was the best way to keep those connections alive when I had a real knotty problem to solve.

A problem like this.

But social connections wouldn't work here.

Only one thing would.

I drew another deep breath and blew out my cheeks. Almost everyone gone. Just me and Sam left.

It struck me then how much I depended on him, how much I feared losing not just his professional support, but his personal presence as well.

I knew I'd put him in a bad spot with the higher-ups and that the tone he took with me was due to that. But I also had to wonder how much of it had to do with my refusing his key.

Sam was mentally strong, emotionally honest and incredibly patient. But he was also only human. It would make sense if disappointment over the key and the lack of progress in our personal relationship affected his handling of our professional one.

I couldn't blame him. Despite everything—despite the hurt I'd caused him over the key and now the trouble I'd put him in with management—he had stood by me. Defended me.

As he'd always done, time and time again.

And, as always, he'd been honest with me, strong enough and brave enough to tell me the truth, even when I didn't want to hear it. I had to appreciate that. I had to—

Hmm.

A stray thought sliced through the guilt, sharp as a paper cut.

Maybe it was a trace of anger I didn't want to acknowledge. It was like a little devil I didn't know I had sitting on my shoulder just up and started talking.

I wasn't being honest with myself.

Yes, Sam was indeed good at telling me truths—about me. But what about his own?

He was top notch at pointing out my choices and my mistakes, the ones I'd made and might be about to make.

But he was very close-mouthed when it came to sharing truths about himself. Oh, he accepted criticism and could be quite self-critical. I liked that about him, but ...

Not for the first time, it occurred to me that one of the things that held me back from Sam was the sense that he lived with shadows, too. If I alluded too much to my past, he referred too little to his. If my home included too many mementos of my history, then his—as attractive as it was— included too few of his. In fact, there was nothing there to speak of who he was, who he'd been before coming to the *Chronicle*. When he first came, there had been gossip, of course, but it ... Well, it amounted to little more than specu-lation. And once he was installed in the position, he proved to be such a good manager that no one ever thought to ask —*anything*. Indeed, no one wanted to.

Everyone was happy with Sam.

Everyone but management.

And that was my fault. Sam's only issues with manage-ment were because of me. The little devil piped down, hushed by the little angel that was apparently sitting on my other shoulder.

With a sigh, I gave my head a little shake and rubbed the back of my neck. This was not the time for meandering musings about Sam's past or self-pity about my present. I had a job to do and I didn't have much time to do it.

What was I going to write? More importantly, how was I going to phrase it?

I picked up a blank sheet of paper and rolled it into my

Underwood. Placed my fingers on the keys, held them there for a second, then took them away.

How could I tell this story without causing more damage, more pain?

Finally, I did something I've done when lost before. I placed my fingers on the keys and closed my eyes. Slowed my breathing. Waited—and sure enough, the words came.

I began to type, slowly at first, then steadier. My fingers fell into a familiar rhythm—as comforting as a heartbeat. The words came like they'd been waiting. And as I wrote, the darkness edged away. It wasn't gone, just held at bay. For then, that was enough.

The click of the keys became a steady rhythm. Each letter struck was a blow against Selena's distortion. Small blows, but deliberate. Measured. Defiant.

At some point, I noticed Sam standing in his office doorway, watching. His silhouette—comforting at first—shifted the longer I looked. Not a guardian or angel. But a watcher. A stranger.

And again that thought crept in: I didn't really know him. Not all of him. In the fading light, I couldn't read his expression. I thought I saw concern. But maybe that was just what I needed to see.

What I *did* see, unmistakably, was the burden he carried.

Focus. Put your head down and finish.

The words kept coming. Slower now. Careful. Each one chosen with precision, not passion. I walked a line—enough truth to satisfy management, not enough to make Seth's troubles worse. It was a tightrope without a net.

Time disappeared. I didn't track it. The rattling of the typewriter was the only sound I cared about. It was my refuge and my reckoning.

Finally, it was done. I set a period at the end of the last sentence. Centered the page. Then pounded out those two words every writer lives for.

—*THE END*—

The big clock on the wall told me an hour had gone by. I ripped the paper from the typewriter and started reviewing the piece. This article held the power to alter futures. I hoped it would quell the firestorm rather than stoke its flames.

Footsteps echoed on the hard wood floor. I looked up to see Sam heading toward me. His gaze met mine, touched with apprehension. I handed him the article, waited as he read silently. I'd never been nervous before about Sam reading anything I wrote, but I could feel my hands turn clammy.

He flipped through the pages, brusque but thorough. Every so often, he'd nod, or raise an eyebrow. After what felt like an eternity, he thrust the article back at me. "It'll do."

No praise, no critique. Just those two words. I sat there, holding the pages, feeling the power of his distance.

He started back to his office without another glance.

12

———

"Sam?" I stood up, calling after him. "Your being upset with me. It's not just about the story. It's the key, too, isn't it?"

He stopped. Turned to look at me. And walked back. His expression was thunderous with disbelief, his gait stiff with anger.

"No. Don't you go there, Lanie. Don't you dare imply that I'd let my personal feelings mess with my professional judgment. That I'd let what goes on out there—" he jabbed a finger toward the windows, the outside world, "affect what goes on in here. I'm better than that. And you know it."

"Yes. Yes, I do. But ..."

"But what?"

"Please, Sam. I'm sorry. For dragging you into this mess. And for ... the key. For being who I am, I guess."

I stood before him, hands clasped, hoping for a forgiveness I probably didn't deserve. His eyes searched mine and whatever he saw there made him soften.

"I understand," he sighed. "I know you want time. And

I've been trying to give it to you. But I'm starting to think time's not the answer, that it's not going to solve our problem."

A stab of anxiety. "What do you mean?"

"I *mean* that this didn't start with the key. That just brought it to the surface. Truth is, I didn't expect you to take it. I didn't expect it—but I hoped you would."

I could've left it there. Let the silence settle into peace. But something in his tone hit a nerve.

And just like that, anxiety turned to anger. "So, it was sort of a test, was it?"

"I wouldn't put it like that, but I suppose you could, yes."

That did it. "Look," I said. "I understand that you might be running out of patience, but as far as I'm concerned, if anyone's out of line, it's you."

"Oh, really?"

"Yes, really. It's you moving fast, not me moving slow. From the very beginning, you've been pushing, pushing."

"Is that right now?"

I was suddenly furious. I didn't know why. At that moment, I didn't care.

"Trust doesn't come easy to either of us."

"Don't turn this around."

"I'm not turning anything. You want honesty? At least, I show my wounds. I have the guts to carry mine up front, right out in the open. You keep yours buried. Like you're ashamed or something. What are you hiding, Sam? What don't you want me to see?"

He froze. The pain that flared in his eyes. It stole my anger and replaced it with regret.

"Sam, I didn't mean—"

He lifted a hand. "You're right. I do have secrets. And

whether you like it or not, you're better off not knowing them. It's safer that way."

Before I could respond, he walked off, shoulders tight, every step final.

13

I stayed away from the newsroom the next day. Worked from home. Sent my articles over with a messenger boy. Then I puttered around the house, took care of other paperwork.

That afternoon, I went hunting.

I found her at Connie's Inn. The restaurant hummed with afternoon quiet. A piano player practiced scales in the corner, the notes drifting like smoke through the emptied nightclub. The place wouldn't come alive for hours yet, when the downtown crowd rolled in looking for hot jazz and cold drinks. But it was the perfect place to conduct a little business.

Selena was toying with a French 75 when I entered, posture relaxed but eyes sharp. True to her habits, she'd chosen a corner table where she could watch both entrances and she spotted me the moment I walked in. Her smile bloomed, all teeth and no warmth.

"Well, if it isn't Harlem's finest," she said as I sat down. "Finally decided to join the party?"

"Cut the nonsense, Selena," I said, sliding the rival newspaper across the table. "Your story is a mess and you know it. Who talked to you?"

Her smile widened as she picked up the paper. "A mess? I'd call it inspired. But I suppose we can't all be perfect, can we?"

"Half the details are wrong. You've sensationalized the incidents and put people's lives at risk. You've got a source and I need his or her name."

She laughed softly, leaning back in her seat. "Straight to the point, as always. I missed that about you, Lanie."

"Tell me who your source is."

She tapped the rim of her glass thoughtfully, her gaze never leaving mine. "Now why would I do that?"

"Because you're smart enough to know when you're out of your depth. That story's making waves, but if it falls apart, so will you. If your source turns out to be the saboteur and someone gets hurt, you could be charged as an accessory. Your editors may love you now, but they won't know your name when this blows up."

Her smile faltered for a second, but she recovered quickly. "Oh, Lanie, always the bluffer. I'm the one holding the cards here."

"Then play them."

She leaned forward. "I'll tell you—on one condition."

I waited. She wanted me to ask. I wouldn't give her the satisfaction.

Finally, she sighed dramatically. "I want back in at the *Chronicle*. Not the obits. Full reporter. And you'll make it happen."

I laughed before I could stop myself. "You're delusional if you think I have that kind of pull."

"You have enough." She lifted her glass, slow and smug.

"Sam listens to you. Your word carries weight. I want you to use it."

I stared at her. "And if I refuse?"

"Then I guess you'll just have to live in the dark." She shrugged.

Her confidence was maddening. I bit back the words that came to mind and forced myself to be noncommittal.

"I'll think about it." I stood to leave.

Her laugh followed me out the door, light and triumphant. "Don't take too long, darling. The offer's only good till your next deadline."

14

Sam didn't look at me when we stepped in. Just stood behind his desk, hands braced on the back of his chair, his focus fixed on Selena. The narrowing of his eyes said plenty—this meeting wasn't his idea.

"Well," he said, "if it isn't Selena Troy. Back to make more waves."

Selena's smile was bright and calculated as she extended her hand. "It's good to see you again."

Sam ignored her hand and gestured to the chair. "Have a seat."

She sat with practiced grace, crossing her legs like she already owned the place. I stayed by the door, arms folded, the knot in my stomach coiling just a little more.

"I have to admit," Sam settled into his own chair, "I was surprised to hear that you wanted to come back."

"Surprised? Why?" Selena tilted her head. "The *Chronicle* has always been my first love."

"That's one way to put it. Your departure wasn't exactly amicable."

Her expression didn't falter, though her voice softened.

"I'll admit, I was young and ambitious—too ambitious, perhaps. But I've grown. My time at the other paper has taught me a lot about the industry."

Sam's gaze went to me—barely—but didn't stay. "Your recent story has certainly made headlines. Though I can't say I agreed with your way of telling it."

She didn't miss a beat. "My style might be considered ... provocative. But it's effective. People read my stories, talk about them. Isn't that what journalism is all about? Engaging the public?"

"Journalism," Sam said, "is about *informing* the public. Engagement is secondary to integrity."

"I couldn't agree more. That's why I want to come back —to bring the *Chronicle* stories that inform, engage and make an impact."

Sam kept his face even, but I caught the tightness around his mouth. He wasn't buying it. Not for a second.

"Selena, you've always had talent. But talent isn't everything. Working here requires trust— trust that you're committed to the *Chronicle's* standards and values. That was an issue before. How do I know it won't be again?"

She leaned forward. "Because I know what's at stake now. I've learned from my mistakes. Let me prove myself. Give me a trial run. If I don't meet your expectations, you can send me packing."

He studied her, clearly deliberating. He'd received orders from upstairs, no doubt. The question was whether would he follow them. The room felt too quiet. Even the newsroom's hum beyond the glass faded.

Finally, he nodded once. "One chance."

They briefly discussed her starting date. Then Selena rose, smile polished sharp. "I won't let you down." She brushed past me as if I wasn't there, a ghost she could walk through—or a corpse she could walk over. I was invisible now that I was no longer useful.

"She'll never name her source," I said.

"I know. But management thought it was better to bring her in than to let her run wild."

"You mean they actually thought it was safer to let the snake into the hen house than—"

"Have you set up the Duval interview yet?" Sam was already reaching for another file, voice clipped, eyes locked on the page. "Mamie's getting harder to pin down. If you've got a date, I need it. If not, I'll send someone else."

I hesitated. Not because of Mamie. Because of him.

"It's set," I said. "Friday. Late afternoon."

"Good." He didn't look up. "This is one interview we don't want to mess up."

I felt the sting of that little barb. Maybe, he didn't mean it the way it came out. But maybe he did. The difference was that before he wouldn't have said it—and if he had, I would've known what he meant by it.

He moved on to the next folder like we'd never had a conversation, like none of it—not Selena, not the key, not the blowup—had ever happened.

I left his office without a word, sat at my desk and thought things over.

Selena Troy, back in the fold.

Not for her redemption. Not for her skill.

Just to keep the poison where we could see it.

And Sam?

He was shutting doors now. One file at a time.

Just to keep the poison where we could see it.

And maybe—just maybe—to see if I'd take the bite.

15

———

After Selena's article broke and my follow-up soon after, Seth banned all reporters from his set and erected a wall of secrecy around it. I tried to keep investigating, hanging around the warehouse, talking to actors and crew members as they left after a day's shoot, but they veered away when they saw me and Seth refused my calls.

It looked like an airtight ship all right. But a determined rat will always manage to chew its way in and Selena managed to slip through.

That very next week, she handed in another story—this one more damning than the last.

The newsroom buzzed as I walked in, typewriters clacking beneath the murmur of conversation. Heads turned my way, expressions ranging from curious to uneasy. Eyes darted toward the stack of freshly printed *Chronicles* on the corner desk.

Selena Troy's byline was front and center.

'*Sabotage or Sabotaged Dreams? Trouble on the Set of Soul Redemption.*'

I snatched up a copy, pulse quickening:

Crew members describe tense working conditions under director Seth Carter, whose mercurial leadership style has allegedly turned collaboration into chaos. Sources close to the production claim Carter's temper has flared on multiple occasions, resulting in public dressing-downs of cast and crew alike. One witness described a scene in which Carter's tirade left an actor in tears. 'He wants perfection,' the source said, 'but he's destroying people to get it.'

It went on like that—an unrelenting takedown of Seth's professionalism. I didn't like her tone—the veneer of concern posing as reporting—but for a split second, I wondered if she'd spotted something I hadn't. Seth had spoken of a crew as close as family. Selena painted a picture of a cruel, abusive director. It didn't jive with the Seth Carter I knew, but apparently, she had sources that I—

"Good morning." Selena slid up beside me. "What do you think? Engaging, isn't it?"

Engaging? No. "Unauthorized."

She raised an eyebrow. "Unauthorized? You mean without Seth's blessing? Since when do we care about that? Anyway, Sam thought it was fantastic. Said it's exactly what the paper needs—timely, provocative and relatable."

"Sam knew?" The words came out sharper than I intended. But even as I asked, I knew the answer. Nothing in our newsroom made it into print without Sam's say-so.

Her smile widened and I hated the satisfaction in it. "Knew? He approved it. Practically rolled out the red carpet. You didn't know?"

I stood there, dry-mouthed. That he'd approved this piece of garbage was bad enough. But that he hadn't warned me? That—

"Lanie?" Selena tilted her head. "You look a little green."

I forced myself to breathe. *Relatable*. She said Sam had

called it 'relatable.' The *Chronicle* had always prided itself on depth and honesty, on nuance, neutrality and integrity. Not this.

Selena's eyes glittered. "Oh, come on. Don't be so stiff about it. You know as well as I do—stories like this keep the lights on. People don't want dull facts. They want drama, conflict and a little dirt with their morning coffee."

"Dirt? Is that what you're calling it now?"

"Truth has many layers, doesn't it? I peel them back, give the public a glimpse. What they do with it—that's not my problem."

I tossed the paper onto the pile and turned my back on her to walk away.

"Loosen up, Lanie. Maybe then you'll finally make the front page."

That stung. Her stupidity. Her arrogance . Her conceit. I whirled around, ready to give her a piece of my mind, but Sam's voice stopped me. It cut through the newsroom. "Lanie. In here. Now."

The din of typewriters and thump of the wire service printers fell away as Sam's office door closed behind me. He gestured for me to sit, but I remained standing, arms crossed.

"I assume you've read Selena's piece," he said.

"I have. And I assume you know how damaging it is to Seth's production."

Sam sighed. "It's not ideal, no. But it *is* compelling. The higher-ups see it as proof she's worth the risk."

"The risk?" The word tasted like ice. "She's quoting

anonymous sources, spinning half-truths, undermining the work we're supposed to be doing."

"She's doing what management wants her to."

"And what's that?"

"Bring attention to the paper."

"Oh, is that our job now?"

"It is, in part and you know it." A beat. "If you have an issue with her reporting, write something to counter it."

I stared at him, chest tightening. I wanted to ask: *Is this how it's going to be now? Because I turned down your key?* But the words didn't come. "You're telling me to compete with her? To stoop to her level?"

He met my gaze. "I'm telling you to prove why you're the best."

The ground tilted beneath me. "You could've told me."

Sam hesitated, just for a beat, but it was enough. "It's not my job to hold your hand." He paused. "I didn't think I had to."

The tightness in my chest spread, curling hot and sharp around my ribs. I knew he was under pressure—could see it in the way his shoulders hunched, the weariness in his eyes. But knowing didn't make it sting any less.

Again, I had to wonder: *Was this about that damn key? Was that why he felt so distant?* I started to ask but caught myself. What was the point? Hurt pride would make him deny it. And the mere suggestion would make him angrier than he already was.

"She's tearing Seth apart."

"It's not our job to protect him."

"It's not our job to destroy him, either. And for what? A few more headlines? A little more buzz?"

"She's got management on her side. Right now, her work is setting the tone. If you don't like it, change it."

I could've said a lot of things, but I left it at one word: "Understood."

His eyes lingered on me, softer now. I sensed that he wanted to say something more. But whatever it was, I was in no mood to hear it.

I walked out. The newsroom's chatter rushed back in a wave, as if nothing had changed. But something in me had shifted and I felt it in every step.

I'd barely reached my desk when my telephone rang, sharp and insistent. I stared at it hard, still seething. *Right on time,* I thought. *Right. On. Time.* I closed my eyes for a second, took a deep breath, then snatched up the receiver. "Hello, Seth."

"Lanie, what the hell is going on?"

"I assume you've seen Selena's latest masterpiece."

"I've seen it. *Everyone's* seen it. Now my crew's looking at me like I'm some kind of tyrant, dragging them through hell for the sake of my 'ambition.'"

"But they know you. They must know she's—"

"It doesn't matter. And it's not just them. It's my investors. The people in the industry. The folks I work with now and hoped to work with later." His words grew sharper. "Don't you get it? Y'all put my picture in the paper. I can't even walk down the street without somebody saying something. People believe this shit. And you know why? Because it's in your paper. The so-called *Times* of Harlem. The paper of record. And I can't even defend myself because I don't know who's feeding her this garbage."

This was my chance. I took it. "You want me to find out?"

A pause. "You can do that?"

"Maybe."

"How?"

"Let me back on set. I can't do anything as long as I'm locked out. You want this fixed? Let me in."

Silence. Tension crackled through the line. "Then what? If I did, what would you do?"

"Talk to your people. Figure out who's talking and what's really going on. If you want the truth out there, you need to let me do my job."

"They're not going to trust you."

"They will if you talk to them, let 'em know I'm not there to just write another hit piece."

More silence, then a sigh. "Fine. You're in. I'll make sure everyone knows they can talk to you."

"One more thing."

"Yeah? What is it?" Cautious again.

"I'll need you to stay out of my way. No hovering. No interruptions."

A bitter laugh. "Don't worry. I've got enough to deal with without babysitting a reporter."

I didn't believe him, but pretended to. "Good."

"But Lanie." He stopped, a beat of quiet before the next words hit. "If you find out who's talking, I need to know. If someone's trying to take this film down from the inside—"

"I'll let you know if I find anything concrete. But understand something—I'm not your spy. If people think I'm a tattle-tale, they won't talk and this'll be over before it starts."

The line crackled with tension.

"You think I don't know that?" he shot back. "Just do what you have to do. But fix this. Because if this film goes under, it's not just my name. It's their livelihoods."

He disconnected.

I stood there, staring at the receiver, before setting it down.

Sam had betrayed me. Selena was running wild. And now Seth was asking me to be something I wasn't—a fixer, a gatekeeper.

His advocate.

It's not your job to protect him.

But what else could I do?

For the first time, I wasn't sure where my loyalty belonged. With the story? Or the people behind it? For the first time, I'd have to make a choice.

16

Seth's office wasn't built to hold four people, especially not four people who didn't want to be there. Seth sat behind his desk, shoulders hunched, hands clenched. Grace perched on the couch, a little apart from him and to his left. Her back was straight, hands clasped on her lap. Clay had given me his desk chair. So I was parked there, uncomfortably aware of the tension in the room. As for Clay, he leaned against the doorframe opposite Grace, jaw set.

Seth was noticeably thinner, his clothes hanging off his large frame and his eyes were dark and sunken. He now looked at us like we'd all let him down. "The investors are on my back. Calling every damn day, asking what the hell's going on."

Clay shrugged. "They're skittish. Angels always are. You'd think they'd be used to a little chaos by now."

"This isn't chaos," Seth shot back. "It's sabotage. And Selena's articles aren't helping. Now we can't control what she writes, but we can control how we respond. Our backers want confidence, not excuses."

"So, what's the plan?" Grace asked.

"First, we need to find out who's talking to her." Seth turned to me. "Lanie, you've got the green light to talk to anyone you need to. Cast, crew, everyone. I've told them to cooperate. Want to use my office for interviews?"

I considered it—for all of thirty seconds. Private might encourage some people to talk. But it might intimidate others into silence. Either way, I'd miss the subtle cues that came with watching people in their natural environment— the quick glances, the offhand comments, the little gestures they didn't know they were making. Besides, it would disrupt production.

"Thanks, but I'll talk to them on-set. People are more themselves in familiar surroundings."

Seth gave a sharp nod, then faced Grace and Clay. "We're tightening the schedule. Grace, I need you need to work with Clay on the script."

"Not likely." She shot Clay a resentful look. "The first thing he'll want to do is cut my lines."

Clay ignored her and spoke directly to Seth. "She'll never cooperate."

Grace straightened up, her fingers drumming against the armrest. "Cooperate? You mean just give in and do as you say, right?" She turned to Seth, her expression sharp. "Why, if it weren't for me—"

Seth raised a hand. "Enough. Both of you. This isn't about your egos—it's about keeping this film alive."

They fell silent, both obviously unhappy. There were family tensions here I hadn't known existed.

"Be flexible," Seth continued. "Anything we can cut, we cut. Anything that makes us faster, we do it."

Clay sighed. "I've already trimmed every scene to the bone."

"Then trim it again. Or combine scenes. I don't care. We're running out of time."

"Okay, okay—but *everybody's* got to be willing to sacrifice." Clay shot Grace a resentful glance.

She gave a cool shrug. "Fine. But don't expect me to carry the weight."

Poor Seth. Investors panicking, Selena stirring chaos and a wife and brother at odds.

Seth's gaze lingered on Grace for a moment, softening. Sam used to look at me that way, in meetings. Now, he looked right through me.

Seth tapped his ear. "Looks like you're missing an earring."

Grace's hand flew to her ears, fingertips brushing the lobes. One of her crystal earrings was missing.

"Hmm. I must've forgotten to put it on this morning," she said. "This whole business has gotten me so turned around, I've been forgetting everything lately."

That seemed so unlike her. Grace was the definition of a star who was cool, controlled, not easily ruffled. It was a small thing, her remark, but it showed me just how much the stress was affecting Seth's people.

"Have there been anymore incidents?" I asked.

"No." Seth shook his head. "It's odd, but they've stopped." He thought about it. "As a matter-of-fact, they stopped right after Selena's first piece came out."

"Really?" I reflected. "I agree. That's odd."

"Do you think the saboteur and the person behind the leaks are one and the same?" Grace asked.

"Maybe," I said. "Maybe not. Could be the same person. Could be the saboteur is simply happy letting Selena do his dirty work for now."

Clay spoke up. "Either way, it doesn't mean the sabotage is over. It could just as easily pick back up again."

"And you still don't want to take this to the police?" I asked.

Seth shifted uncomfortably. "No. The last thing we need is cops swarming the movie set."

Clay grunted. "Swarming? No such luck. They'd either ignore us—or shut us down."

"Neither of which would solve our problem. We've got enough trouble as it is."

Grace and Clay both murmured their agreement.

Seth let out long exhale and lightly slapped his desk, a sign that the meeting was over. "All right then," he said and looked at me. "Lanie, it's your show now. Do what you do best."

Grace walked with me a bit after we left Seth's office. She reached out and gently touched my arm, her eyes searching mine. "You will find out the truth about this, won't you?"

It was a question I'd heard before. "No promises, but yes, I'm pretty sure I will."

She was silent a moment. Then she looked back to Seth's office, where we could see him once again bent over paperwork. Her chest rose and fell with a sudden, shallow breath. Then, as if pulling herself back from a thought she didn't want to share, she looked at me again. "Have you ever had a dream that consumed you? A dream that you would do anything to see realized?"

Sure, I understood the desire to excel beyond everyone's expectations. Lived with it every day. But to "do anything" to see it realized? No, I didn't understand that. Not at all. It struck me that she chose that phrasing. And it struck me even more that she was looking at Seth when she said it.

"Yeah," I nodded. "I get it."

A whisper of sadness floated across her face. "But sometimes, those dreams come at a cost. Sacrifices must be made. Choices that ... one might come to regret."

She touched the bare earlobe briefly, then let her hand fall. Her gaze drifted back to Seth before returning to me.

I waited for her to say more, but she just shook her head and walked away. I glanced back at Seth—still hunched over his desk. Was Grace trying to protect him—or warn me about him?

Or was it both?

17

The summer heat trapped by the warehouse roof made the air thick and sluggish. Seth said he'd told his cast and crew they could talk to me. But permission didn't guarantee candor. I couldn't blame them. With all the ink being spilled about Carter and the accidents, every word they said to a reporter could come back to bite them.

I started with the actors. They sat in folding chairs at the far end of the set, scripts in hand. Most found their pages suddenly fascinating when I approached.

A woman with dark hair and sharp eyes cut me off before I could speak. "No comment."

A young actor nearby shrugged, script dangling from his fingers. "I keep my head down. Whatever happened, it's above my pay grade."

The others kept their heads buried in their lines. I jotted down a few notes, though none of it was worth much.

The lighting crew was next. Two electricians coiled cables near a rig, their hands moving steadily while their eyes stayed on their work.

"What do you make of the incidents on set?"

One glanced up briefly. "Things break. It's a set."

The other shrugged. "Could be coincidence. Could be carelessness. I don't know."

"Would it take someone with specialized knowledge to cause those kinds of problems?"

The first man paused. "Depends. The rigging failures? You'd have to know what you were doing to mess with that without getting caught."

"Or getting hurt," the second added.

"Who knows the equipment best?"

The two exchanged a glance before the first one said, "Well, that'd be Westbrook. He's been at this longer than any of us."

The second nodded. "Yeah, he knows his stuff. Cameras, lights, the works."

"Would he have reason to cause problems?"

"No way," the first one said. "Westbrook's a professional."

"Not even if he was frustrated?"

"Westbrook gets frustrated every other day," the second said with a faint smile. "But he doesn't take it out on the job. He's old-school."

I jotting down their answers. "About Selena Troy. Did either of you talk to her—or any other reporter?"

The first man snorted. "Not a chance."

"Got enough problems without that," his partner said.

Their answers felt about as useful as a broken camera lens. But I thanked them and kept moving.

Everywhere I went, the answers were the same—short, vague and deliberately unhelpful. That old wall of silence, built from bricks loyalty, fortified by fear.

A group of grips stood near a stack of crates. Their laughter was loud enough to turn heads over the whir of electric fans and the distant clatter of set construction. The youngest—the same kid who'd interrupted my interview with Seth—stood with his hands jammed into his overall pockets. He was trying to look tough, his expression somewhere between defiance and embarrassment as the others teased him.

"C'mon, kid, let's see it again." That was an older guy, wiry with grease-stained hands.

The kid hesitated, then pulled out a small square of pink cotton. It was delicate, with embroidered roses dotting neat little loops on scalloped edges. Very feminine.

"Damn," the wiry man laughed. "How much you blow on that thing? Week's wages?"

"Close enough." The kid managed a sheepish grin. "But she's worth it."

The others roared. A broad-shouldered man clapped him on the back. "Hmm-hmph! That little sheba's sure got you by the short hairs. But man, you gotta know she's way outta your league."

"Yeah? Well, maybe she's not. You don't know her."

The wiry man snorted. "Don't need to. You think shebas like her go for guys like you? Keep dreamin'."

"You're just jealous," the kid shot back, chin up.

"Sure. Whatever you say. But she's probably laughing at you right now."

I cleared my throat, stepping closer. The laughter died quick and the men shifted as they noticed me. The kid shoved the handkerchief back into his pocket like it was contraband.

I introduced myself, said why I was there. "Got time for a few questions?"

"Sure," the broad-shouldered man said, but he didn't sound like it. The others hung back, suddenly finding interest in their boots or the rafters above—anywhere but me.

"What do you make of everything that's been happening on set?"

"Stuff happens," the wiry man shrugged. "Could be bad luck. Or someone not paying attention."

"You think it's deliberate?"

The kid stared at his shoes. "Uh, I dunno."

"And Mr. Carter? How's he handling it?"

"Yeah, he's wound pretty tight," the broad-shouldered man said. "But can't blame him none. Man's trying to keep this whole operation from falling apart."

"Like any good boss," the wiry man added, wiping his hands on his overalls. "Rather have someone riding us hard than picking up the pieces later."

I thanked them for their time, then went looking for Westbrook. Behind me, their teasing started up again, voices lower but still rough with humor.

I spotted Westbrook near the main camera, talking with a woman. Pretty but plain, a sparrow among peacocks. Navy dress, scuffed shoes, gray hair pulled severe, a practical handbag slung over one arm. She had the weathered look of someone who counted pennies and long days. She wasn't part of the cast or crew. I could tell that much.

Westbrook was showing her something on the rig, gesturing with one hand while she nodded. She didn't seem impressed, exactly, but focused, matching his intensity.

"Take care, Sydney," I heard her say. "Looks like you're carrying quite a load."

Westbrook grinned and for a moment he looked like

whatever man he used to be. "Don't I know it? I'll see you later." There was a quick hug—friendly enough, but something more intimate lived in the gesture. Then she walked away, giving him a small wave of goodbye. Her gaze lingered on him like she was afraid she wouldn't see him again.

Westbrook turned, his grin fading when he spotted me. He folded his arms. "Mrs. Price. Here to ask more questions?"

"Selena Troy."

"What about her?"

"She's been busy. And she seems to know a lot about what's happening here."

He nodded, a spark of anger in his eyes. "And you think I'm feeding her."

"Someone's talking. Not just about the sabotage. They're quoting Seth. Word for word."

His gaze darkened. "It's not me."

"You sure about that?"

"You think I'd risk everything I've put into this film to run my mouth to Selena Troy?"

"Sometimes people say more than they mean to—especially to someone like her."

He let out a sharp breath. "Some do but not me. I know how people like her operate. They don't ask questions—they dig for ammunition. I wouldn't give her the time of day."

No hesitation in his words, no guilt in his eyes. But guilt was tricky—it didn't always show its face when you went looking for it.

"What about the sabotage?" I asked.

"What about it?"

"You're saying you've got nothing to do with that either."

His thick arms tightened across his chest. "I told you

before—I wouldn't sabotage my own investment. Why're you asking me the same damn questions again?"

"Because people dig a lot of dirt for a lot of reasons. Maybe out of spite. Or jealousy. Maybe just to prove a point."

Westbrook didn't answer right away. His jaw tensed; the veins in his temple pulsed. The world shrank to just the two of us. Everything else—voices, footsteps—faded away. "Spite? Jealousy? That's what you think this is about?" His lips curled into something too sharp to be a smile. "You really don't know a damn thing about what's going on here, do you?"

"Then fill me in, why don't you??"

His eyes drilled into mine, weighing me. Deciding if I was worth the trouble. The hum of the rig grew loud in my ears, filling the pause, louder than it had any right to be. The big man stepped closer, his broad frame blotting out the light.

"Let me be clear. I don't have time for this nonsense and I don't need to defend myself—not to you, not to anyone. I've worked too damn hard on this film to see it fall apart now. You want to chase ghosts? Be my guest. But don't drag me into it."

The silence that followed was as sharp as his words.

"If you're innocent, I'll leave your name out of it. But if you're lying, I'll find out."

Westbrook held my gaze, eyes black as nitrate, then turned back to the camera as if our conversation had never happened.

I watched him work for another moment before turning to leave. If he was hiding something, he was good at it. But good wasn't the same as perfect.

It went on like that, interview after interview. Wall after wall. Meanwhile, I had to keep up with the usual round of parties and club meetings that were the steak and potatoes of my column. The regular entertainment editor stayed out sick, so I did a review of *Good Trouble,* Bella Crain's latest vaudeville hit. She was a jazz singer and making it big. Some said she'd be bigger than Florence Mills. I didn't know about that, but I had to agree that she was dynamite.

Nothing more untoward happened on the movie set. Either the saboteur had decided to let Selena do the heavy lifting or possibly, but less likely, her articles and my questioning had scared him off. I wish I could say I believed the latter. But I didn't. I had a feeling we were all waiting for the next shoe to drop.

And it did.

I just didn't realize we'd be the ones to drop it.

18

Sam called me into his office two days before the next issue went to press. The afternoon light slanted through the blinds, catching the faint wisp of smoke rising from the cigarette balanced in his ashtray. A typed draft of Selena's latest article was on his desk, marked up with blue pencil edits. Her headline was unmistakable:

A Betrayal of Blood: Carter's Vision or Division?

He handed me the copy. My hands shook as I read it.

Seth Carter's films have always been celebrated for their raw, unflinching portrayal of Negro life in America. But behind the camera, Carter's own words reveal a more troubling picture—one of division, blame and bitterness.

"This is us. Our reality. ," Carter said in a recent conversation, "We turn on each other. Not always for greed. But the damage is the same. We stab each other in the back, do at least as much damage as Mr. Charlie. In fact, we often do Mr. Charlie's work for him."

These words, spoken by a director whose work depends on the trust and collaboration of his community, cut deeper than any script. They lay bare a perspective that not only criticizes but condemns his people, turning the mirror inward and shattering it in the process and blaming them for their own oppression.

The words blurred into smudges of black ink. Seth's quote—how had she gotten it? She'd quoted it word-for-word. And stripped it of context, twisted it into an accusation, a dagger and then stabbed deep.

The article framed Seth as an opportunist, not a filmmaker reflecting hard truths, but a cynic profiting off his people's pain while privately deriding them.

"It's trash," I said. "She's actually managed to produce something worse than the last two articles combined."

"That quote," Sam said, tapping the paper with his blue pencil. "Does it sound like him?"

"Yes. It's actually from my interview with him."

"You mean he actually said that? And you knew it but didn't use it?"

"Yes. And for the same reason I held back on the sabotage. I knew how it would sound."

"Once again, Lanie. He's a grown-ass man. Our job— *your* job—is not to protect him."

"Maybe you're right, Sam and Maybe I was wrong, but the point is: that quote? I didn't give it to her."

"Then how did she get it?" He paused, his gaze sharp. "Or is he out there, saying the same thing to other people? If so, then your attempt to protect him was noble but foolish."

"I don't believe he's doing that."

"Well, you'd better make sure. 'Cause the article's running."

"Can't you stop it?"

He laughed, short and dry. "I can't stop this anymore than I can stop a freight train. Look, Lanie, you think I like this? We're in the business of selling papers, not making friends. Management loves it. They're calling it bold journalism. Says it's already doubled our sales."

"That still doesn't make it right."

He held up a hand. "I know, but—"

"If you can't kill it, at least frame it honestly."

He sighed, rubbing the bridge of his nose. "Do you really think Selena's twisting it?"

"You know damn well he didn't mean it the way she's making it sound."

"Never met the man. I know no such thing."

"Well, I have and I do. And what you do know is that Selena doesn't care about nuance or context. Just headlines."

Sam rubbed his jaw. "She says she called Seth to get his reaction. Gave him a chance to clarify."

I raised an eyebrow. "And you believe her?"

He looked up, hesitated, then dropped his gaze back to the desk. His fingers twitched near the cigarette in the ashtray, but he didn't pick it up.

For me, that was answer enough.

I looked at the copy in my hand and felt an urge to slap him with it. Instead, I settled for tossing it back on his desk.

This article would hurt Seth, but it wasn't just him. It was all of us. Every time a colored voice was twisted into something ugly, it gave Mr. Man one more excuse to ignore the truth.

I walked out, my footsteps sounding hollow. My pulse didn't slow. I had a call to make.

I had our switchboard put the call through as soon as I reached my desk. My pulse quickened with each ring. When Seth came on the line, I explained what was what. After his initial shock, his response was as expected.

"You want to tell me why she has my words, Lanie?"

"Seth, I didn't give them to her. I—"

"Then how does she have them? I said those words to you, here in my office. We were alone. No one else was here. So how, Lanie? How?"

"I don't know." My grip tightened on the phone. "But I swear, it wasn't me. You have to believe me."

"Do I? You're the only person I said those words to. The only one. I trusted you. Do you know what this could do to me? Those words—twisted like that—they're a weapon now."

"She didn't get them from me."

"Then how does she have them?"

Good question. No one else had been in the room. No one. Just he and I.

"I don't know," I said again. "All I can say is, now's your chance to comment."

A tense pause stretched long enough to make my chest feel tight.

"Why should I? So, your paper can twist those words, too?"

"No, Seth. It's not like that. It's—"

"Then how is it?"

The line went dead. The silence felt louder than his voice had.

_____

19

S elena was at her desk, typing away like she didn't have a care in the world. When I slammed her article down in front of her, she barely glanced up.

"Ah, you've read it." Her lips curled with a smirk. "What did you think? Gripping, isn't it?"

"You're out of control. Do you have any idea what you've done?"

"What I've done ... is my job." She sat back in her chair, picked up the pink silk handkerchief lying next to her Underwood. "Something you might want to try sometime. This story needed to be told."

"This isn't a story," I shot back. "It's gossip. Speculation. And it's hurting people—real people."

Her smirk didn't falter. "If Seth Carter's so fragile that he can't handle a little bad press, maybe he's not cut out for the big leagues." She threaded the handkerchief through her fingertips like an executioner playing with a noose.

"You don't care who you hurt, do you?"

"Care doesn't pay the bills. And frankly, Lanie, if you'd done your job, I wouldn't have had to step in. You had the chance to break this story weeks ago, but you were too busy protecting your precious Seth."

I stared at her, shaken. The truth of her words hit me in my gut. She wasn't entirely wrong—my loyalty to Seth had made me cautious.

But that didn't justify what she'd done.

"You'll regret this," I said, turning to leave.

Selena's voice followed me. "We'll see about that."

20

As Sam said, the *Chronicle* was a key newspaper in Harlem. A story attacking a prominent Negro filmmaker in its pages was bound to generate intense local reaction—and it did. Unfortunately, newspaper management underestimated what kind and how much.

The phone calls started the minute the paper hit the streets and they poured in from every corner of the community. Civil rights leaders, church pastors, theater owners who showed "race films." Other Negro artists and intellectuals weighed in, along with regular folk. Even the colored businesses that advertised in the *Chronicle* had their say.

The reaction split sharply. Some defended Seth, saying he was speaking plainly. Others saw his words as a betrayal.

"This is our moment in the sun," one caller said. "And he's telling white folks we're stabbing each other in the back?" Another called him worse than a race traitor—"a Negro who gets successful then turns around and spits on his own people."

Some thanked the *Chronicle* for "telling the truth" about Seth. Others condemned us for "putting it out there." They worried Selena's article would affect Harlem's cultural movement, feared the division would play into white hands and jeopardize future Negro film productions.

Through the newsroom din, I caught fragments of operators' conversations at their switchboards:

"Yes, Reverend, I understand your concerns—"

"No, ma'am, we stand by our reporting—"

"The Lincoln Theater? Yes, I'll have someone call you back—"

Sam's office door stood open. He sat at his desk, phone pressed to his ear, scribbling notes. His ashtray overflowed with crushed cigarettes. He waved me in without looking up.

"I understand completely, Mr. DuBois." He listened, face tight. "Yes, the Chronicle has always supported our artists, but—" Another pause. "I appreciate your position. We'll take it under advisement."

He hung up, only for the phone to start ringing again. This time, he didn't answer.

"That's the third movement leader this morning," he said, rubbing his temples. "Actors, crew members, their friends and relatives—all of them furious. And that's just Seth's side."

"And the other calls?"

"The Lincoln Theater's threatening to pull their investment in the film. Three other theaters say they won't show it when it's done. Ministers are warning their congregations to steer clear of Carter's work and Marcus Garvey's people are calling this proof we need our own distribution networks." He shuffled through message slips. "And someone's organizing a protest at the set.

Sam looked up at me with tired eyes. "Go ahead and say it."

"Say what?"

"That you warned us. That we should've shut Selena down. Never should've hired her."

I thought about it. Sam had green-lit Selena's piece. He should've seen the fallout coming. Maybe he had. If so, he'd chosen to stand back, let it hit. For a brief moment, I wondered if he'd done it on purpose, given Selena—and management—enough rope to hang themselves. But that was probably just wishful thinking. The fact was he hadn't just failed to warn me. He'd chosen not to. He'd let that story run; now he was in a jam and wanted my help in getting out of it.

"I admit it," I said. "'I-told-you-so's' are always tempting. But how would that help?"

I moved to the window, watched people hurrying past on the street below. "We're all in this mess together now." I turned to face him. "The question is, what are we going to do about it?"

21

That was the night I started following Selena. It wasn't a decision I made lightly. Spying on a fellow reporter was a line you didn't cross. But this wasn't about a byline anymore—it was about the truth. And that truth was getting buried alive.

I watched her slip into Darleen's Fish 'n' Fry diner late that evening. I waited across the street in my car. No one joined her. No furtive conversations. No whispers over coffee. I followed her to Miss Vicky's beauty salon on 125th the next night. Nothing.

Meanwhile, she was busy. Goodness knows what she was up to, but I had the feeling that time was running out. Following her was turning out to be both ineffective and inefficient. Too hit or miss. Time for a more direct approach.

The phone records came next—a step I rationalized with grim determination. I sweet-talked one of the *Chronicle's* operators into letting me take a peek at the call logs.

Nothing there either. No connections. No smoking gun. Just a tangle of numbers that could mean everything or nothing.

Somehow, word got back to Selena. She stormed into Sam's office to complain, her voice loud enough to cut through the din of the newsroom.

"Sam, do you know what she's been doing? Checking my call logs? And I bet she's been following me, too."

"Got any proof of that?"

"No, but it's something she'd do. Dog my heels like some two-bit detective."

Sam got up and went to his door. His gaze caught mine, lips tight, then he shut the door and pulled the blinds. Their conversation went silent, but you could still see their shadows. I've got to say, it was quite a show and just about everybody stopped to watch it. Selena's anger, Sam trying to calm her. He must've promised her something—'cause she walked out five minutes later wearing a smile like a loaded gun.

Sam came to his door and beckoned me in. I felt Selena's eyes drilling into my back, hers and everyone else's.

The door shut behind me with a thud. Sam didn't sit, just leaned against his desk, arms crossed.

"You want to tell me what's going on?"

"I'm trying to find her source."

"By spying on her?" He shook his head. "That's not how we do things here."

"Someone on that set is feeding her information and that someone could be our saboteur."

"Or just a disgruntled crew member with an axe to grind."

"Either way, they're using Selena to spread lies. And she's letting them."

He studied me. "I understand why you did it. But there's a right way to get at the truth."

"And what if the right way isn't enough?"

He didn't answer immediately. We both knew what was at stake. Finally: "Write it clean, Lanie. But if you get this wrong ..." He didn't finish the sentence, but he didn't have to. His eyes said it all.

I nodded, but my gut churned. Clean stories didn't always make it to print. And sometimes, the ones that did left the real story to rot in the dark.

As I left Sam's office, Selena's gaze caught mine. Her lips curled into that same loaded smile. I could feel it—this wasn't over. Not for her and not for me.

If the truth was buried, I'd just have to dig deeper.

But before I could, I got a message. It came an hour later.

Management wanted to see me.

22

The publisher's office was stiflingly warm. Sunlight streamed through the tall windows, casting sharp angles across the walls. The room was not small, but it felt close. The heavy mahogany conference table dominated the room. The air was stagnant and hard to breathe. The faint smell of ink and paper lingered, a reminder of the lifeblood of the *Chronicle* just outside these walls.

Leonard Maxwell, the king cobra—or, in everyday parlance, the publisher—sat at the head of the table. He was solitary and secretive. And he reigned over the paper with reptilian intelligence and Machiavellian manipulation.

He was flanked by Joelle Evans, the managing editor and Exeter Hughes, head of business operations. Evans ... so deceptively soft and round. She reminded me of a rabbit—harmless, cuddly—right up to the moment she sunk those buckteeth into you, teeth that could shred steel.

If Evans was a deceptive rabbit, Hughes was a vulture in plain sight. All bone and angles, with a neck that craned slightly forward, as if always scouring for the dead or dying. His skin had the sheen of scorched bronze, tight across high cheekbones, darker at the temples where the scalp showed through. Eyes close-set, with the dry gleam of someone who knew the cost of everything and the value of very little. Hands like claws—bony, precise, always folded or poised to strike. His suits fit like feathers: sleek, dark, silent. He was the silent listener, watching, waiting for weakness to show. Cold and circling, he cared only for one thing—stripping profit from the bones of a story and leaving the rest to rot.

Sam sat to my left, his posture rigid, hands clasped in his lap. He didn't look at me. He was right next to me, but there might as well have been a chasm lay between us and it felt unbridgeable.

My notebook lay untouched on my lap. I didn't need to take notes—I already knew this would be a meeting I wouldn't want to remember.

Maxwell removed his glasses, set them down with deliberate care. "Miss Price, Mr. Delaney—thank you for making time. We won't keep you long, but this is a discussion that can't wait."

Sam nodded once. There was a certain weight to his silence—I could feel him holding back—like a storm contained behind a wall.

"We've reviewed the recent coverage of Seth Carter's production," Maxwell continued. "Selena Troy's stories have driven readership numbers—strong ones."

I glanced at Sam. Caught a flash of annoyance. No— something more. Much more.

"They've also generated controversy," Sam said.

Evans crooked an eyebrow. "You have a problem with that? Since when? Since when do we shy away from controversial subjects?"

The hypocrisy. This paper had avoided controversy for

as long as I could remember. And everyone in the room knew it.

"This isn't about controversy or the fear of it," Sam said. "It's about intellectual honesty." He paused. "And journalistic integrity. Her stories have crossed the line when it comes to both."

There was an audible gasp—and God help me, I think it was from me.

Evans drew herself up, insulted. Her words snapped, like a rabbit's bite when cornered. "Say what you will about Miss Troy, but her reporting has been bold and courageous. She's not afraid to go after the tough stories." She pointedly looked at me.

I had some choice words for her, but I knew that's what she hoped for, to provoke me into saying something they could use against me. Sounds paranoid? You'd better believe it. With this bunch, I had every reason to be. So I kept my mouth clamped shut. But inside, my thoughts sizzled and I gave full vent to my anger. *Bold and courageous?* Twisting quotes and sensationalizing tragedy wasn't courage—it was opportunism.

Evans wasn't done. "Miss Price, your reporting, while solid in the past, has left us with some concerns lately. We understand you withheld information about the sabotage on Mr. Carter's set. Can you explain why?"

I took a deep breath. "Mr. Carter asked me to delay reporting on the sabotage to give him time to have it investigated."

"Did he tell you he'd brought in the police, that the incidents were under active investigation?"

I squirmed. "No, he—"

"Did he not, in fact, tell you he had not reported it to the police and didn't intend to do so? Did he not, in fact, ask you to keep quiet about the sabotage so it wouldn't scare away his investors—thus making it clear that his main concern was money and his film rather than the safety of his cast and crew?"

I glanced at Sam for support, but his gaze stayed locked on the table. "At the time," I said carefully, "I believed that delaying the story would serve the greater good. It allowed Mr. Carter time to investigate the matter internally and—"

"It allowed ... the problem to continue, even escalate. This was a matter of possibly criminal activity, one that put lives at risk. Yet you said nothing."

He was, perhaps, right. I couldn't find the words to respond.

"Did Mr. Carter promise you anything in exchange for your silence? An exclusive?" Maxwell paused, his tone sliding into something darker. "Something else?"

Heat crept up my neck, but I forced my expression to remain neutral. I wasn't entirely sure exactly what he was implying, but the general import was clear—and mortifying. I fought the instinct to stiffen or recoil. Both would've given him exactly what he wanted.

"No." My voice was calm, deliberate. "Absolutely not." I looked him in the eye, though my hands clenched beneath the table. The insinuation lingered in the air, slimy and insidious. But I wouldn't let him see me flinch. "I made my decision independently, based on my judgment as a reporter."

Evans was unimpressed. "You are aware that reporting isn't about curating the truth, Miss Price. It's about presenting it—warts and all."

I forced myself to meet their gazes. "I've reported what I believed to be accurate and responsible. The situation on set is complex and I've made it a point to avoid sensationalizing it."

"'Sensationalizing,'" Maxwell echoed, raising an eyebrow. "Is that what you think Miss Troy has been doing?"

My chest tightened. "I think Miss Troy and I have different approaches to reporting."

"Approaches, perhaps," Evans said. "But her work has been thorough, unflinching and, I dare say, courageous. She's not afraid to dig into the harder truths and it's resonating with our readers."

"Miss Troy's reporting may resonate," I said, "but it also distorts. She—"

"We're not here to dissect her methods. We're here to discuss yours," Evans said. "This isn't the first time you've taken positions, made decisions, that were ill-aligned with the success of this newspaper."

Maxwell chimed in. "The *Chronicle* has a responsibility to its readers. We're in the business of informing the public, not protecting those who may be endangering it. Miss Troy understands that."

My stomach churned, but I stayed silent. Beside me, Sam spoke, finally said something in my defense.

"Miss Price has consistently upheld the highest standards of journalistic integrity. Her track record speaks for itself. If her choices seem conservative compared to Miss Troy's, it's because she prioritizes getting it right."

Maxwell's gaze slithered toward Sam, deliberate and unblinking, a snake honing in on momentarily forgotten prey. "And you, Mr. Delaney—you supported Miss Price's decisions?"

Sam straightened, though I could see the tension in his shoulders. "I trusted her judgment, as I always have. She's one of our most dependable reporters and her instincts have rarely led us astray."

"Rarely," Maxwell repeated, his tone dry. "But the *Chronicle's* reputation can't rely on past successes." His gaze sharpened. "Let me be frank: there's a perception, whether fair or not, that you've given Miss Price too much leeway because of your ... personal connection."

The accusation landed hard. Sam stiffened. "My relationship with Miss Price has no bearing on my editorial decisions."

"Perhaps." Hughes tilted his head, a vulture weighing whether the remains before him were worth the effort. "But perception matters—to our readers, our advertisers and this paper's bottom line."

Evans nodded, her gaze darting between the two of us, quick and twitchy. "We can't afford even the appearance of favoritism."

Sam's jaw clenched; his frustration showed in the sharpness of his voice when he spoke again. "We've made our positions clear. Let's move on."

"I'll say when it's time to move on!" Evans slapped the table with the flat of her hand. "Now, both of you have done fine work in the past—work we've been proud to publish. But that doesn't mean your positions are guaranteed. Understand? If this lack of judgment continues, the *Chronicle* will be forced to reevaluate where you fit into its future."

The words hit with a finality that was undeniable. This was really why they'd brought me and Sam into the room. This was the message they'd intended to deliver all along. It didn't matter what we said or could've said. The questions were all rehearsal. This was the real show.

Maxwell broke the silence, his gaze shifting back to me.

"Do you have anything else to say for yourself, Miss Price?" Another question that was a mere formality.

I lifted my chin. "Only that I stand by my choices. My priority has always been to tell the truth, not to chase headlines." I paused, then delivered my own blow. "If that is no longer valued here, then I'll need to re-evaluate my place as well."

The room tensed. The rabbit gasped and clutched her pearls at the effrontery. Sam shot me a brief, sharp glance. The others exchanged looks, their faces stony. None of them responded directly.

"Very well," Maxwell said, standing. "You two now have your chance to prove yourselves. Miss Price, you'll need to deliver follow-up pieces that are thorough and fair. No omissions."

"Yes, sir," I said.

"We'll deliver," Sam added.

"Good," Maxwell said. "For your sakes, I hope you do."

The hallway felt too narrow as we walked out. I could still feel Maxwell's cold eyes coiled around us and Hughes' gaze lingering, confident his prey was now weakened, just waiting for it to stumble.

I waited until they were out of earshot before speaking. "What are we going to do?"

Sam didn't look at me. "Well, I, for one, am going to do my job. I suggest you focus on yours."

My jaw dropped. "What does that mean?"

He finally turned to me, eyes hard. "It means," he said with gritted teeth, "that when someone's trying to put you in the grave, you don't offer them a shovel. What the hell were you thinking? Saying you'd re-evaluate your position with the paper? After everything I've done, continue to do, to convince them of your loyalty?"

I took a step back from him. His words cut deeper than anything those managerial midgets had said—or could've said.

"Everything *you've* done? What about me, about the thousands of hours I've logged, the hundreds of stories I've filed? The cases I've broken that the police couldn't—or wouldn't—touch? I've done more than proven my loyalty. Time and time again. I don't need you to—"

"No, you don't need me. You never have. And you make sure to remind me every chance you get."

He turned away before I could answer, his back stiff as he walked away, leaving me standing there, stunned, alone and feeling utterly on my own.

23

It was mid-morning when I woke up. My curtains kept the harsh morning light out, but it couldn't fully prevent the heat from seeping in. I blinked, eyes gritty and feeling damp from a night of fitful sleep. The emptiness beside me felt more pronounced than ever.

I dragged myself out of bed, every movement an effort. The floorboards creaked under my feet.

In the bathroom mirror, a stranger stared back at me. Dark circles under her eyes, .

"Pull yourself together, Lanie," I muttered.

I mechanically went through the motions of getting ready for work. As I applied lipstick, I remembered how Hamp had sometimes come in and stood behind me, watching me prepare for my day.

"You look beautiful, darling."

I'd laughed then, carefree. "Flatterer."

Now, the echo of his voice twisted like a knife in my chest.

I gripped the edge of the sink, knuckles pale. The urge to curl up and hide from the world was overwhelming.

But the world wouldn't wait. Stories needed writing, truths uncovering.

I straightened my shoulders, met my own gaze in the mirror. The woman looking back was a shell, but she'd have to do.

I dressed and headed downstairs. Breakfast was one slice of toast with jam and two cups of black coffee. It wasn't enough and I knew it. Later, my stomach would gripe and I'd feel like I was running on fumes. But for now, it was all I could manage.

I grabbed my purse and headed for the door, but I didn't go to the newsroom. Instead, I hid behind two society club meetings I regularly covered and a third I did not. Truth was, I was trying to avoid Sam. I just didn't have the energy to face him.

It was mid-afternoon by the time the meetings were done. I headed back to Strivers' Row, thinking I'd write my column from home.

But my feet had other ideas.

They carried me past my townhouse and across the street. Carried me the way grief does—quiet, unannounced. The scent of my neighbor's garden reached out, touched me —crushed geranium leaves and sun-warmed soil floating on the hot air, a perfume no department store could bottle. I found myself standing at her gate, fingers curling around the iron just to feel something solid.

Gladys Cardigan had buried two husbands and lost two sons to the Great War. Forty years teaching Harlem's children had earned her a place in the neighborhood's heart. These days she poured that same nurturing spirit into community service and mentoring. If anyone knew about surviving grief, she did.

Gardens were as rare as a poor man lot on Strivers' Row.

The limestone townhouses that lined our street left no room for nature's softer touches. But Mrs. C had created her own green oasis of paradise. Terra cotta pots marched up her limestone steps and clustered beside the stoop, spilling pink petunias and purple geraniums toward patches of sun between the brownstones.

She was working among the ground-level planters, apron dusted with soil. Her hat tilted back from her brow, revealing the thin braid she always wore looped around her head like a crown. Her gloved hands were patting the soil around a marigold like a mother tucking in a child.

"Afternoon, Mrs. Cardigan."

She looked up, shielding her eyes from the sun. "Afternoon, yourself. How're you doing, sweetheart?"

"I was hoping to talk for a bit, if you have time."

"Of course. Come on in, child."

She straightened up, slow and careful, brushing her hands on her apron before gesturing She gestured to a small iron bench next to her coleus and impatiens. It was a perfect spot for a quiet conversation.

I stepped through the gate and the street noise fell away. Just like that. The rumble of cars, the shouts from stoops, all muffled like someone had thrown a heavy blanket over the world. In Mrs. C's garden, even Harlem knew to lower its voice.

"Just let me wash my hands," she said. "I'll be right back."

She clomped up the front stairs and disappeared inside. I sat stiffly on the iron bench, feeling like a guest who didn't know whether to stay or slip away.

The marigolds nodded in the breeze. Made me think of my father. He'd planted them every spring, said they kept the bugs away from his vegetables. 'Tough little soldiers,' he called them. Funny how a mind files away little things like that. Saves them for later, when they might make sense.

A church bell chimed somewhere a few blocks away. Didn't know which one. Didn't matter. In Harlem, you're never more than a stone's throw from salvation, if you're looking for it.

Minutes later, Mrs. C returned carrying two glasses of iced tea on a small silver tray, the kind kept polished for church ladies and Sunday callers. The ice clinked softly as she set the tray between us.

"Here." She handed me a glass. "Might help chase off that storm brewing behind your eyes."

I took the glass, the coolness startling against my palm. Sipped. The tea was strong, sweet, with a slice of lemon floating on top. And she'd added something extra, something that gave it a little kick.

We sat a while, sipping without words. The marigolds bobbed in the lazy breeze, bright and unbothered.

"I'm sorry to barge in like this."

"You haven't barged. You're always welcome."

I glanced down at the rim of my glass, watching the condensation bead and run. "I'm not sure what I'm doing anymore. I keep thinking I've made peace with things. Then something catches me sideways. Reminds me I haven't."

Mrs. Cardigan waited patiently.

I traced my fingertip around the rim of the glass. "Sam offered me a key. To his place."

I sensed her gaze on me soften. "I didn't take it."

She didn't nod. Didn't frown. Just let the words hang there like laundry on a line.

"My house still feels like... Hamp's," I added. "I'd feel like I was betraying him if I gave another man a key to his house."

"Did Sam actually ask you for one?"

"Well, no, but—"

"You assume he expected you to give him one."

I nodded. "I'm so tired of him pushing me. He should've known better. Why'd he have to go and put me in that position?"

Mrs. C cut her eyes at me. "Yes," she said. "How could he do that? How dare he push you to live and not bury yourself in house like it's a mausoleum?"

I had to smile, a little anyway, at the way she was teasing me. Then I started to respond but she held up a finger.

"First," she said. "It was never just Hamp's house. It was yours, too. And now that he's gone, it's *all yours*. That's number one. Number two is this: Maybe Sam's not the one you're really angry at."

Stunned and puzzled, I drew back. "Excuse me."

She didn't answer right away. Her gaze got soft and distant.

"Funny thing about grief," she said. "It doesn't follow the rules. Not time. Not sense. Not manners."

She took a sip of her tea.

"I remember," she went on, "when my first husband died. Henry. Fool man got himself kicked by a milk wagon, trying to cross Seventh Avenue with two arms full of groceries and no sense."

I gave a weak laugh.

"People think I've always been ... well, comfortable. But back then, I had two babies, no savings and a landlady who raised the rent before the week was out. I ironed shirts, cleaned houses, waited tables—all of it, just to keep us from falling through the cracks."

"And now look at you," I said, gently.

"Second husband had steadier luck." She smiled faintly. "Put his savings into this house just after the war. Said he wanted me to have a place where nothing could be taken away." She paused, gathering a few petals from her apron. "Of course, the second husband got taken too. That's how life works."

I didn't know what to say to that.

"People kept asking if I missed Henry. If I was lonely. I said yes, of course. But the truth?" She looked at me then, meeting my gaze. "I was mad as hell."

I blinked. "Mad?"

"Oh, yeah. Mad he left me with two babies and a roof that leaked when it rained. Mad he didn't hold on tighter. Mad he didn't listen when I said he looked tired and to stay home that day." She took another sip.

"I wasn't supposed to be mad, though. Not a good widow. A good widow mourns and smiles and wears black without causing trouble." Her voice was dry, almost amused. "I did all that. And I cursed him under my breath every time the roof leaked or the baby got sick and there was no money for medicine."

She fell into silence, giving me the space to respond. But I couldn't. My throat locked up.

"I've never been angry with Hamp," I said finally. "I just miss him."

She didn't argue. Just tilted her head, studying a patch of geraniums.

"You sure that's all, sweetheart?"

I swallowed hard. Some part of me wanted to snap back yes. Wanted to say it sharp enough to silence the question. But I didn't. I just sat there, feeling something curl tight in my chest. Something I didn't want to name.

She nodded, as if she believed me, but smiled as if she

knew better. "Grief's a trickster. It don't always wear the face you expect."

The garden smelled of sun-warmed stone, damp earth and something sharper underneath—rosemary, maybe, or marjoram. The air tasted bitter in my throat.

"I should get back," I said, standing too quickly.

She rose more slowly. She touched my elbow in passing, light as a whisper.

"You know where to find me."

I nodded, but my feet felt heavy as I crossed the street.

Home waited—quiet, clean, unchanged.

But for the first time, I wasn't sure I wanted it that way.

24

Selena's articles were expertly woven together, threaded through with truths, half-truths and speculations, so tightly interwoven that an outsider wouldn't know where one thread ended and another began. But to this insider, one thing was clear: she couldn't have written them without help—especially that last one. Seth's words had been private. No one else had been in the room when he uttered them.

How had she gotten them? My first thought was my desk drawer, where I kept my notes between interviews. Could she have rifled through it? It wasn't impossible—I never kept it locked.

I checked. Everything was there, undisturbed. I pulled out the notepad I'd used for that interview and flipped through it. My shorthand was meticulous, each word carefully recorded. But as I compared my notes to Selena's article, a chill crept up my spine. Her piece included details I hadn't written down. Bits of phrasing, context, even emphasis. It was as if she'd been in the room, listening.

For a moment, I considered the unthinkable. Could Seth

have leaked his words himself? Could he have used Selena to spark controversy—a desperate move to create buzz for the film? But no. When he'd made that comment, I'd seen the look in his eyes. He'd known it was risky, but had trusted me to use his words responsibly.

So how had Selena gotten the quote?

I went over that scene again and again, trying to recall every detail. Played it like a movie reel in my mind. Roll tape. Roll tape. Us, sitting there, talking. Me, notepad in hand. Him, explaining, hands gesturing. Him—

The realization hit me, sharp and hard. She hadn't stolen or copied my notes. She hadn't needed to. She'd had eyes and ears in that room, all right.

And I was sure I knew whose.

25

Wilkes sat hunched in the chair, his cap crushed in his lap, looking anywhere but at the two of us. Seth stood behind his desk, arms crossed, shoulders squared. I perched on the edge. My notepad stayed in my purse. Sometimes, a notepad kills a conversation—puts up walls. This was one of those times.

Seth spoke first. "Why'd you do it, Wilkes?"

Wilkes leaned back. "I don't know what you mean, Mr. Carter."

"I'd like to believe you. I really would, but ..." Seth picked up the folded copy of the *Chronicle* from his desk and tapped the front page. Selena's article glared back—bold, brutal.

Wilkes gave it a glance, then looked away. "I don't know nothing 'bout that."

"Sure you do," Seth said. "She couldn't have written that without help from someone on this set."

"It wasn't me. I—"

"Mrs. Price and I kept thinking about how that quote came from a private moment. Just the two of us in the room.

Then she remembered—you came in to deliver a message—"

"And then I left."

"You walked out. But did you walk away? Or did you wait outside and listen?"

Wilkes licked his bottom lip. "You're bluffing."

"Are we?" I said. "Let's talk about the handkerchief."

His head snapped up.

"It was pink with red roses. I saw you showing it off last week. You said it was for a lady friend. Then, a few days later, Selena showed up with one just like it."

Wilkes shifted. "So, what? Bet there's lots of scarves like that."

"Stop," Seth said. "You're making it worse. The fact is, you've been talking to Selena Troy. Spying. Feeding her stories."

Wilkes rubbed his throat. Cornered. He knew it. His eyes dropped to the mangled cap, fingers working the brim like it held answers.

"Wilkes," I said. "Let's go back. Who approached whom? Did you go to her, or did she come to you?"

"She came to me. I didn't go looking for her. And I didn't know she'd twist half the things I said."

It started with harmless chatter—tensions on set, flare-ups between Seth and Westbrook. Then came the mishaps. Rigging failures. Lighting issues. Before long, she'd pushed him to eavesdrop. Wanted gossip about Grace. Clay. The crew.

I wish I could say I was shocked. But I wasn't. It was vintage Selena.

Wilkes clutched the cap. "I didn't think I told her anything that'd hurt the production."

Seth leaned in. "You gave her my words. She twisted

them. Now investors are threatening to walk. Even if I finish this film, no one may screen it. You know why? People are talking boycott."

"I didn't mean for that to happen," Wilkes said. "I swear, I didn't think she'd go that far."

"But you saw what she did with that first article," I said. "Then came the second."

"And you still kept talking," Seth said.

Wilkes didn't answer. Just crushed the cap tighter.

"Let me ask you something," Seth said. "Do the others feel the same way? Is everyone this fed up with me?"

Wilkes' head shot up. "No, sir. It's not like that."

"Then what is it? Did she promise you something? You bought her that handkerchief. Were you two—?"

"No!" Wilkes shook his head. "It weren't like that."

I raised a brow.

"I mean, yeah, I liked her. Too much, maybe. But she never promised ... nothing like that."

"So what did she offer?" Seth said. "Why talk to her at all?"

Wilkes sagged. "She made it sound like she could help. Said if folks knew, you'd have to listen. Things would change."

"What things?"

He hesitated. "The long hours. The low pay. Hauling lights around busted rigs, wondering if one's gonna drop on your head."

"So you had a problem with me," Seth said. "You thought selling me out would fix it?"

Wilkes winced. "No! I just—I wanted you to see what it was like."

"Then why not come to me?"

"Truth is ... people are scared."

"Of me?"

"Someone had to say something."

"And you decided it would be you," Seth said. He looked rattled, like the ground had shifted under him. "Why didn't you come to me? Say something?"

Wilkes exhaled, the fight draining out of him. "She told me she just wanted to help. Said if people knew what was happening, you'd have to listen. That maybe it'd make you think twice before running us into the ground."

I narrowed in. "What exactly did you want Mr. Carter to do?"

"I—I don't know. Something." He rubbed a hand across his face. "It wasn't just the accidents. I told her about Charlie. How you fired him."

Seth's brow knit. "Charlie? This is about Charlie?"

"Who's he?" I asked.

"Best friend I had on this set," Wilkes said. "And Mr. Carter fired him like he was nothing. Yeah, he drank a little—"

"More than a little," Seth said.

"But you knew that when you hired him. He gave everything he had to this film. And you tossed him aside like trash."

"I let him go," Seth said, "with more money in his pocket than he'd seen in a month of Sundays. Because he was a risk —to himself and everyone else."

"Charlie tried. He really tried."

"And everything he touched had to be checked twice. You know that, Wilkes. Because you were the one doing the checking. I saw you. Following him. Watching him."

Wilkes flinched and turned away. "I don't want to talk about Charlie no more."

"No, I guess you don't," Seth said. "But you could've talked to me. About him. About all of it."

Wilkes looked up. Eyes rimmed red. And just like that, he wasn't a man anymore—just a kid, wounded and worn. "Really? When? When do you ever have time for us?"

That hit Seth. Hard. His crew was supposed to be family. Close-knit. Unbreakable. Now it looked like he'd missed more than he'd realized.

Wilkes turned to me. "Ma'am, maybe you'll understand. Miss Selena said I was making a difference. Said I was brave."

"Brave," Seth said, bitter. "Sneaking around. Spying. You risked everyone's job—mine included—to make me the villain?"

Wilkes flared. "I told you—I didn't mean for it to go this far. I thought—"

"That's the problem," I said. "You didn't think. You trusted someone who doesn't care about you or this crew. She used you. And now we're all paying the price."

He slumped. "I know. What I did—it was wrong. You asked why I kept going. Truth is, I liked her. I thought she liked me. After that first article, she promised not to be mean no more. And I—I wanted to believe her. But after the second article, I knew. I told her I was done. But she ... she wouldn't let go."

I believed it.

"Let me guess," I said. "She said if you stopped, she'd out you."

Wilkes nodded, eyes down.

He looked pitiful. But pity was hard to come by. He'd complained about low pay, then did the one thing that might've cost everyone their paycheck. Complained about one man getting fired—then risked the whole crew getting shut down. I didn't know what irked me more: the gullibility or the blind short-sightedness.

"So tell me," Seth said. "What else did you do?"

The air changed. I hadn't expected the question—but I should have. It was the next step. And it had to be asked.

"Was it you?" Seth said. "Did you do it?"

Wilkes looked stricken. His mouth opened. Shut. Then opened again. "N-no, Mr. Carter. You gotta believe me. I know it was stupid, talkin' to her. I knew even while I was doing it. But I'd never—never sabotage the set. Please believe me."

Seth exhaled through his nose. Long. Slow. He leaned on the desk and stayed there, silent. Thinking.

Then he looked at me. A silent question.

Call me a fool, but I believed Wilkes. I saw it in Seth's face—he did too. Maybe he was second-guessing himself, unsure if he could trust his own gut. I knew that feeling. But not today.

Wilkes was young. Foolish. But not malicious. And not smart enough to rig a sabotage scheme.

Seth straightened. "You know how much damage you've done?"

Wilkes nodded. "Yes, sir."

"You're lucky I'm not throwing you off this set."

Wilkes blinked.

"But you're on notice. One more screw-up and you're out. Understand?"

"Yes, sir. I swear—it won't happen again."

Seth was pale. He pinched the bridge of his nose, then stifled a cough against his sleeve. "All right," he waved a hand. "You can go."

Wilkes stood, holding what was left of his cap. "I'm sorry." Then he left, closing the door with a soft click.

Seth stood still for a second. Then his shoulders dropped. He collapsed into the chair.

"He didn't do it," I said. "The sabotage."

"I know." Seth rubbed his face. "But that's tomorrow's problem." He picked up Selena's article and tossed it at me. "This is today's."

"She's gone, but the damage stuck."

"The film's hanging by a thread. Half my investors are ready to bolt."

"So what now?"

"Damage control. I need to meet with them. Try to stop the bleeding."

"What'll you tell them?"

"That we found the leak. That it's handled?" He shook his head. "Words won't cut it anymore."

He stood, pacing. "I could show them what we've shot. Let the footage speak for itself."

"A rough cut? That's a risk."

"My films always are."

"And if they hate it?"

"Then they were leaving anyway."

He looked at me—drained, hollow. The man who faced Wilkes was gone. What sat before me was someone watching his dream bleed out.

"I'll be there," I said. "I'll write what I see. What they see."

His hope faltered. "And if it's not enough?"

Good question.

Outside, clouds rolled in. Heavy. Gray. The kind that promised a storm.

We didn't say it, but we both knew:

If the investors pulled out, it was over. The film, the jobs, the dream.

All of it.

26

Darlene's Fish 'n Fry was nearly empty, the way it always was between lunch and supper. A couple of old-timers nursed Cokes at the counter and Darlene herself was behind the register, balancing receipts and listening in without looking.

We had the corner booth. A pitcher of iced tea sat between us, already half gone. Seth sat across from me, both hands wrapped around a sweating glass he hadn't touched. Oscar Micheaux sat beside me, his glass half empty and full of lemon slices.

Micheaux was in his early forties, already a legend. *The Homesteader. Within Our Gates. The Conjure Woman.* His films gave us a mirror—not the degrading version Hollywood fed the world, but something closer to truth. He showed us as we saw ourselves. Not just in relation to whites, but to each other. The frictions. The expectations. The fight to rise without dragging one another down.

"Selena Troy," Micheaux said. "I've read her work. She's got ambition. I'll give her that."

"Ambition?" Seth's repeated. "She twisted my words into a weapon. And the *Chronicle* printed it."

"She's clawing her way up," I said. "And she's doing it the easiest way she knows how—by tearing someone else down."

"Doesn't make it right," Seth said. "Her latest piece? Worse than the first. Took something I said, made me sound—"

"Bitter," Micheaux cut in. "Angry. Divisive." He gave a dry shake of the head. "Old trick. Use the truth like a knife. Doesn't mean you have to let it carve your name."

"I'm not letting it. But it's poisoning everything. Backers are spooked. Crew's whispering. I'm supposed to clean up her mess when I should be finishing this film."

He wasn't wrong. But locking himself away, pretending silence was strength, wasn't helping. I'd brought him here hoping Micheaux could break through that wall.

Everybody agreed that Seth's idea of doing a screen was a good move--but it wouldn't be enough.

"The story's out there now," I said. "Ignoring it won't make it disappear."

Seth pressed his palms into his forehead. He looked worn down—his frame leaner than it should've been. The kind of wear that came from too many nights solving problems no one else could see.

"So what?" he said. "Fight her in print? She's got the *Chronicle* behind her."

"Not entirely," I said.

Micheaux turned to me, one brow raised. "Go on."

"My editor's under pressure. Management loves the sales Selena's bringing in, but they're also fielding blowback. Readers are pushing back. Especially those who support Seth. It's... delicate."

"Delicate." Micheaux let the word sit. "That's one way to put it."

Seth coughed into his handkerchief, then folded it up slow. "Maybe I should just wait it out. Say more and she'll twist it again. Feed the fire."

"No," Micheaux said. "You own it."

Seth shook his head. "What the hell does that even mean?"

"It means you stop letting her frame it. You've got something to say. So say it."

"The truth?" Seth said. "You mean the quote she twisted into a lie?"

"I mean the truth behind it," Micheaux said. "You said disunity's a problem in our community. That's true. But the answer isn't to bury it. Name it. Confront it. That's what your film's about, isn't it?"

Seth didn't answer right away. The fight in his eyes dimmed. Still there, though. "Yeah," he said. "It is."

"Then lean into it. Selena's version of the story is small. Yours doesn't have to be."

"Easy for you to say. You're not on set every day, holding this thing together while folks wonder if you're the problem."

"You think I haven't lived that?" Micheaux asked. "Every project, someone says I've gone too far. That it won't sell. That I'm wasting money. But I keep going. Eyes on the prize. That's the only way through. You've got vision, Seth. Don't let her reduce it."

"Look," I said. "Fighting her in the papers isn't the only way." I paused. "But it *is* one of the best."

Seth narrowed his eyes. Micheaux did too.

"Lanie?" Micheaux said. "You've got a plan?"

"I do." I leaned in. "It's risky, but if we play it right, we won't just flip the story—we'll make Selena wish she'd never picked this fight."

27

———

The newsroom buzzed with the low murmur of typewriters and the occasional ring of the phone, but that day there was an undercurrent of tension on top of the usual. Word had spread fast: Seth Carter was on his way. Every eye darted to the clock or the entrance. Whispers flitted between desks—speculation, nerves and excitement.

When the clock struck the hour, the door swung open and Seth Carter strode in. Heads turned, conversations flatlined and typewriter keys stilled mid-strike as Seth cut a path through the room. He looked every inch the director who didn't just make race films but defined them.

Sam stepped out of his office and extended his hand. "Mr. Carter," he said. "Welcome."

Seth shook his hand. "Mr. Delaney. Thank you for agreeing to see me."

Sam's gaze shifted to Selena and me. "Miss Troy. Mrs. Price. Please join us."

Sam and I had been walking on eggshells around each other since that meeting with management. Professional territory, that was. We'd patched things up enough to work together. But the personal tension between us? That was another matter entirely.

Selena rose smoothly from her desk, her chin held high. She was always composed, but her shoulders were just a little stiffer than usual. I followed, my notebook read. Seth's gaze rested on Selena for a moment before locking back onto Sam. It was his first good look at her. And, as the saying goes, if looks could kill, she would've dropped dead on the spot.

Sam's office wasn't small, but it felt cramped with all of us in there. Seth took the seat opposite Sam's desk, his posture relaxed but his gaze intense. Selena perched on the armrest of the couch, the small rose handkerchief clutched in her hand. I leaned against the wall, notebook in hand while Sam eased into his desk chair.

"I'll get straight to the point," Seth began. "I came here because I'm tired of being misrepresented. "Miss Troy, your articles didn't just take my words out of context—they butchered them. Twisted them into something unrecognizable."

Selena tilted her head, her lips curving into a faint smirk. "I'm reporting the truth, Mr. Carter."

"Are you?" Seth shot back. "You call it reporting, but you're not chasing facts—you're chasing fire. And it's my life, my people, you're putting the torch to."

Sam held up a hand. "Now, let's keep this civil—"

"I am being civil," Seth interrupted. "But I'm also here to defend my work. What Miss Troy is doing doesn't just hurt me—it hurts the people working on my film, the crew who depend on this production for a living. She's sowing division where there wasn't any."

Selena stiffened, her smile still in place but her voice just a beat slower than before. "If your crew is divided, that's not my doing. I report the reality, Mr. Carter, not your fantasy."

"Your 'reality' is whatever gets you the most attention. But at whose expense? Who pays the price for your version of the story? You sell scandal like it's your currency, but don't pretend you're doing anyone a favor. People's livelihoods— this community's trust—it's not yours to gamble with."

Selena didn't flinch, but something in her shifted—a tension in her shoulders, a hint of irritation she couldn't quite mask. Her good looks and confidence had always been her armor—impenetrable and polished to a shine. But even armor dents if you strike it hard enough and Seth Carter had found the weak spot.

Sam shifted, his gaze dropping for a beat too long. That pause said everything. The way he shifted in his chair, his jaw tight—it wasn't mere embarrassment. It was shame. He was a man caught between two fires—his fealty to management and his understanding of the truth. Sam, the independent journalist, might've once agreed with Seth, been ready to acknowledge that Seth wasn't wrong. But Sam, the paid editor, the company man, couldn't say so, not out loud.

"I came here because the *Chronicle* has a responsibility," Seth continued. "Not just to sell papers, but to serve the community. Miss Troy's articles might sell, but they're burning bridges in the process. And when the smoke clears, the *Chronicle's* reputation will be right there in the ashes." He cleared his throat, a rasp that seemed to linger longer than it should and his chest rattled faintly when he exhaled.

Sam opened his mouth, but Seth wasn't finished. "I'm

not asking for favors. I'm asking for balance. For fairness. If the *Chronicle* is as committed to truth as it claims to be, then it should tell the whole story."

The room was silent and suffocatingly close. Even I was finding it difficult to breathe. Small, glistening beads of moisture now dotted Selena's forehead. She dabbed them away with that handkerchief, her posture tense and straight.

Sam, meanwhile, looked like a man remembering that he used to stand for something. He glanced at the plaque on his desk, the one that said, "Truth First." Maybe it reminded him of a time when truth wasn't something to negotiate—and he not only had a voice but the guts to use it. Maybe it gave him strength.

Sam leaned forward, hands clasped like a man searching for control. "I hear you, Mr. Carter. But interpretation isn't ours to govern—we report and the rest follows."

"Maybe not. But you sure as hell control the lens you use to frame it."

Sam's head snapped back, as though Seth's words had landed a blow. The muscles in his jaw worked, the tendons in his neck standing out, but he didn't argue. Couldn't.

I realized then that I had no idea what it was like to be in his shoes. It was easy for me to criticize, to stand back and say what I would've done in his shoes. I had Sam to protect me from the ire of management. Who did he have? No one. No one was standing by his side. When he stood up to the powers-that-be, he stood alone.

Seth had one more point to make, one more nail to drive home. He demanded an interview—"a fair one. With the reporter of my choosing."

Sam shot me a look. To Seth, he said, "We'd be more than happy to interview you again, sir, but—"

"But nothing. You've had your chance to tell my story.

Now I get to take mine." For good measure he added. "I've got people ready to boycott your paper. Make *you* the center of the story—and not in a nice way."

The room was silent.

Sam's gaze dwelled on Seth, eyes reflecting a pain and sympathy he couldn't express. Finally, he exhaled and nodded. "You've made your point, Mr. Carter."

Seth rose, smoothing his jacket, his gaze lingering on Sam for just a breath. Not in pity. Or with anger. Just the quiet assurance of a man who'd won. He turned and nodded to me. "Mrs. Price." Then he looked past Selena as if she didn't exist.

He left. Sam walked to the doorway of his office and stood there, watching Seth go. I could imagine what he was thinking: that one of the hottest young Negro directors alive had just been to his office—and it had not been to applaud the job the paper was doing.

The newsroom fell silent. Eyes darted from desk to desk. Someone coughed and the sound cracked through the room like a gunshot. No one moved. No one breathed. Then the whispers started—low murmurs like ripples spreading across still water. Someone dared to ask, "What the hell just happened?"

Inside the office, Selena stayed seated, pale as cheese, arms folded across her chest, the handkerchief balled up tight in her grip. "Sam, this visit of his—it was proof—"

Sam silenced her with a glance. "Selena, leave."

Her lips pressed into an unhappy, bloodless line. For a moment, I thought she might argue, but instead, she rose, smoothing her skirt with a jerky motion. She didn't look at me or Sam as she left, her heels clicking too sharply against the floor.

I started to leave, too, but he shut the door. He went back

to his desk and leaned on it as if it were the only thing holding him upright. Then he turned to me, rubbing his temples. "Lanie," he said, "let's talk."

28

He didn't move from his desk. Just looked at me, like he'd been waiting for this moment since the day the first article dropped. I stayed near the door, arms crossed, unsure whether to sit or stand.

"You want to talk," I said. "Fine. Let's talk. Start with why you let her print that garbage."

His jaw flexed. "Management backed her."

"You could've pushed back."

"And you could've written the damn story when you had it. Instead, you sat on it. Gave her the opening."

"You could've pushed back."

"And you could've written the damn story when you had it. Instead, you sat on it. Gave her the opening."

I flinched. Just slightly. But enough that he saw it. And when he did, he didn't back off.

"That's not fair."

"No," he said, "it's not. But it's true."

He came around the desk, pacing now. "You want to know how she got in? You cracked the door. You left it wide enough for her to slip through. And once management saw the numbers on her first article, that was it. They wanted fire. You gave them a bucket of silence."

"I was trying to do right by Seth."

"And I was trying to do right by this paper."

His voice lowered, but the heat stayed. "You think I didn't want to protect him too? You think I didn't want to back you up? But when it came down to it, you made a promise you couldn't keep. Then you acted like I was the one who let you down."

He stopped pacing. Just stood there, staring at the floor, like he couldn't figure out where the ground went.

"I begged you to cut her loose."

"Yes, but you made it harder for me to do it."

I stared at him, stunned. Hurt didn't even begin to cover it. "So this is all on me?"

"I didn't say that."

"You didn't have to."

He ran a hand over his hair, fingers shaking. "This job— this newsroom—it's held together with thread. Every day I fight to keep the wolves at bay. And I do it knowing I could be pink-slipped at any minute."

He looked away, then back. "You know what management did after that meeting? They hauled me in there alone, said you'd gone soft. That maybe I had too. That if they could replace you, they would—and they'd replace me right after. They'd cut me loose the minute I stepped out of line."

That landed like a slap. I stared at him. "I thought I was the reason they were gunning for you."

His smile was bitter. "You were the excuse. Not the reason."

That silence between us opened wide again. But this time it wasn't cold. It was scorched earth.

I folded my arms across my chest. "You should've told me."

"You should've written the damn story."

He had a point and I knew it.

"You're supposed to be my ally," he said. "Instead, you keep going rogue, making judgment calls that leave me exposed. And now you want to stand here and ask why I didn't fire her?"

We were silent for a long moment. The noise from the newsroom crept back in—typewriters, phones, the low murmur of voices. It all sounded so far away.

"I trusted you, Sam," I said.

"I trusted you too."

I looked at him. Really looked. The tired eyes. The slumped shoulders. The weight—no, the burden—of every choice we'd made, every thing we hadn't said. It was all right there between us.

I nodded once. "I guess we both failed each other."

He didn't respond. Just walked to the window, hands on his hips and stared out like the answer was somewhere in the city haze.

I stood there, unsure what else to say. Then I turned to go.

He didn't stop me.

But as I reached the door, I saw it—just a trace in the glass pane's reflection.

He'd braced both hands on the window frame, shoulders bowed—like something in him had finally cracked.

I froze.

Just for a second.

Then I looked away. Whatever I might've said—might've felt—stayed locked behind my teeth.

He hadn't meant for me to see it.

And I couldn't unsee it.

I stepped into the hallway, closed the door gently behind me and kept walking.

There'd be time to feel things later. Right now, I had an interview to prepare for.

29

S elena Troy was used to shaping the story. But Seth Carter had done something she couldn't: he'd made the truth impossible to ignore. And now, the rest of us would have to reckon with it.

Seth and I met for the interview in the *Chronicle's* conference room. It was a quiet enclave to one side of the bustling newsroom. The faint clatter of typewriters and the busy murmur of conversations seeped through the glass walls, but here, the focus was singular.

Seth sat across from me, dressed in a tailored suit. He looked every bit the visionary filmmaker: poised, deliberate and here to reclaim his story. He appeared calm, but his hand trembled slightly as he reached for his water glass.

The formality of the conference room underscored the formality of our meeting. I gave him a faint smile and he gave me a slight nod. We both knew what was what. I couldn't hold my punches and he needed to respond with honesty—knowing that *everything* he said would be considered on the record.

"Thank you for coming, Mr. Carter."

He inclined his head. "Thank you for the opportunity."

I opened my notebook, meeting his gaze. "There's been a lot of recent reporting about your film and its production challenges. I'd like to give you the chance to address some of those concerns."

Seth took out his handkerchief, coughed into it, then folded it away. A slight flush crept into his cheeks as he nodded again. "I appreciate that."

I checked my notes. "Let's start with the obvious: the film itself. There's been a lot of talk about its themes. What's the story you want people to hear?"

It was an easy enough question, a good lead-in. Open-ended, one where he could speak freely—and get his message across, regain his backing and his audience, convince people that his was a story worth telling—or lose them permanently.

"The story I want people to hear is the one we're telling on screen. It's not about me—it's about the community. Our struggles, our triumphs, our contradictions. *Soul Redemption* isn't just a story—it's a mirror. And sometimes, what we see in the mirror isn't comfortable. It's what we don't want to face. But that confrontation? It's necessary."

His hands shook ever so slightly as he clasped them tightly in his lap, steadying them.

I chose my words with care. "One of the film's central themes is disunity. That's been ... polarizing for some. What's your response to critics who say it's divisive?"

He took a breath, deep but strained, as if the air wasn't quite reaching his lungs the way it should. His gaze stayed focused, but there was a brief pause before he spoke.

"I can see how some people might be upset by what they've heard. But what they've heard isn't the whole story."

"What is then?"

He took a moment, then his eyes filled with some remembered pain.

"Disunity," he said, "is a reality we face, but acknowledging it is the first step toward healing. *Soul Redemption* isn't just about disunity, pain and betrayal. It's about hope and love—and resilience, too. It's about where and how we find the strength to forgive and move on—move forward. No, these are not easy topics. Of course, they're not. But they are necessary ones."

Time to challenge him, to play Devil's advocate.

"Some might agree with you there, that it's necessary to explore these issues. But they'd disagree with *how* you're going about it. For example, some might say you're exposing our weaknesses to white people. There's concern that you're worsening our problems, not easing them."

He shook his head, frustrated. "The film isn't about pointing fingers—or airing dirty laundry. It's about starting a conversation. If we don't confront our challenges openly, we can't hope to overcome them."

"Do you think people are ready for that conversation?"

"They need to be. Because if we don't start asking those questions, we'll never find the answers."

"So you don't care how audiences will react?"

"Of course, I do. I care what people think, how they feel, how my films make them feel. But I also believe audiences are more receptive than we give them credit for. People are yearning for authenticity—for stories that resonate with their experiences. If the film sparks dialogue and encourages introspection, then it's fulfilling its purpose."

He'd already answered my questions about the story itself but what about his motives for telling it? That expression on his face, the one in which he seemed haunted by a memory, intrigued me. Had I really seen it there? "Your passion for this project is clear. What drives you personally to tell this story?"

A faint smile touched his lips, but it didn't reach his eyes. "I've seen what happens when stories go untold—voices silenced, experiences overlooked. And I've seen what happens when we wait too long to tell them. This film is my chance—maybe my one and only—to shed light on the truths we can't afford to leave in the dark. It's about empowerment, understanding and ultimately, unity. But we don't have all the time in the world to get there."

"Let's shift to the production. There have been reports of incidents on set—equipment failures, injuries and other setbacks. Some suggest it's due to poor equipment or mismanagement. How do you respond to that?"

Caution touched his eyes. "Film production is inherently challenging. We're pushing boundaries with limited resources and sometimes things don't go as planned. But my people have met every setback with resilience and determination."

"Speaking of, do you have any concerns about your crew? How do you respond to accusations that you've risked their safety for the fulfillment of your dream? "

A hint of anger flashed in Seth's eyes, but he had no doubt expected this question, perhaps even wanted it. His expression remained calm and he answered smoothly. "The picture is important, of course, but the safety and well-being of my crew are paramount. We're doing all we can to ensure that."

"Do you believe these incidents are purely accidental?"

He paused briefly before answering. "Let's just say, we're looking into them. I won't speculate without facts."

His words were carefully chosen, as they should've been, but I couldn't let this go without addressing one of the main issues. Doing so would've done more harm than good—to both of us. We had danced around the subject long enough. Time to broach it.

"There are whispers of possible sabotage. Is that something you can comment on?"

Seth's nostrils flared ever so slightly. "Sabotage is a serious allegation. If someone is intentionally trying to undermine our work, that's not just an attack on me but on everyone involved in this project. We're cooperating with the authorities to get to the bottom of any suspicious activities."

A nice, safe answer. Safe and acceptable. And basically the only response he could give under the circumstances. It was the kind of response that would normally satisfy most people. But these circumstances weren't normal. Selena's articles had whipped up so much public ire....

Should I push Seth even harder? If I printed these answers, would he come across as too polished, too controlled? Would people think he was hiding something or knew more than he let on? Or would they accept his responses at face value, feel reassured that I'd asked enough hard questions—and that he'd answered as honestly as anyone in his position could?

From the corner of my eye, I noticed movement through the glass walls. Selena Troy hovered just outside the conference room, her posture rigid, her face tight with anger. Her eyes darted toward Seth, then to me, as if she were trying to read our lips, decipher what was being said.

I rose and crossed the room to the window. For a moment, Selena and I locked eyes. Then, without a word, I closed the blinds, shutting her out. The light in the room softened, the outside world fading away. When I returned to my seat, Seth raised an eyebrow but said nothing.

Seeing Selena made my mind up. Whatever hesitations or qualms I'd had about whether I'd been hard enough on Seth vanished. If anything, Selena's very presence had made it clear: the truth would come out through the work itself—not through me trying to nail him to the wall. And maybe, just maybe, I could give him one last chance to connect with the audience he was so desperate to reach.

"One final question, Mr. Carter," I said. "If your audience could take away just one thing from this film—just one truth—what would you want it to be?"

Seth coughed again, a harsh, sudden sound. I noticed his shoulders ride up, his posture stiffening as if he were trying to hold himself together. This should've been the moment he was most at ease. The interview was almost over.

He frowned, thoughtful. "I want them to know," he said finally, "that this film is more than a production—it's a meditation—on who we are, where we've been and where we're going. I want them to believe ... in the people bringing it to life and in the impact it can have. Challenges are inevitable, but they don't define us. How we respond to them does."

It was a good response. Inspirational. Giving. Bound to soften some and win back others.

"Do you have any message for those who are skeptical of your work or methods?"

His gaze didn't waver. "I invite them to watch the film when it's released. If they want to know the truth, they'll find it in the work—judge it on its merits, not on rumors or partial truths. Let the film speak for itself."

I smiled slightly. "Fair enough."

Glancing at my notes, I realized we'd covered much ground. "Is there anything else you'd like to add?"

He paused, his voice softening. "Just that I'm grateful for the chance to share my perspective. Open dialogue is important and I appreciate you facilitating that."

"Thank you for your time, Mr. Carter."

He rose, adjusting his jacket and extended his hand. "Thank you, Mrs. Price."

His grip was firm, his expression calm, but as he released my hand, I saw something in his eyes that puzzled me. There was gratitude, yes and a quiet resolve. But that resolve was edged with defeat and something deeper—something more complex. In that moment, despite his outer confidence, Seth Carter looked like a weary soldier, determined but burdened, entrusted with a message he feared might never be heard.

"Here's hoping this gets people talking," he said. Then, with a faint, ironic, almost wistful smile, he added, "That's what stories are supposed to do, aren't they?"

After he left, I walked back to the blinds and reopened them. Selena Troy sat at her desk, leaning on it, her head bent as she rubbed her temples in slow, deliberate circles. As I watched, she straightened up, opened a drawer and drew out that pink and rose handkerchief. She stared at it for several long seconds, her pretty face twisted with frustration and disgust, then threw it into her trashcan. She rested her elbows on her desk again, her forehead cradled in her hand. If I read her right, Selena Troy knew she was looking into a future she couldn't control—or escape.

For weeks, she'd shaped the narrative, casting Seth as the villain. But now, with this interview, he'd taken the first step toward reclaiming it.

He'd shamed the *Chronicle* into giving him this moment,

forced the paper to acknowledge the cracks in its own integrity. But his real battle wasn't here—it was out there, on the screen, where the truth would either break him or set him free.

30

The Chronicle hit the stands late that night. Seth Carter's exclusive interview dominated the front page, accompanied by a striking photograph of him on set, his face lit by the glow of a spotlight. Beside it ran a powerful letter to the editor from Oscar Micheaux himself —a bold move that reverberated across Harlem.

Unity and Disunity: A Call for Honest Reflection

To the Editor of the *Harlem Chronicle*:

I write in response to recent coverage of director Seth Carter and his ambitious film *Soul Redemption*. As someone who has worked to elevate stories that matter to our community, I feel compelled to address the controversy stirred by his words—words that have been taken out of context and turned into a weapon against his character.

Let me say this: unity is our strength. But to achieve unity, we must first confront the realities that divide us. Pretending that disunity does not exist is as dangerous as fueling it. Mr. Carter's remarks reflected a truth we cannot ignore: that our struggles are not only external but internal. This doesn't mean we're doomed to betray one another. It means we can choose not to.

I commend Mr. Carter for facing hard truths. And I ask our readers to do the same. We don't need another generation of artists stifled by fear. We need a generation that dares to speak.

Art is a mirror. It shows us who we are—good, bad, in-between. *Soul Redemption* holds that mirror steady. It asks hard questions, not to divide us, but to draw us closer.

The *Chronicle* doesn't just report news. It shapes the way we talk to one another. Sensationalism sells papers. It doesn't serve the greater good. I urge the *Chronicle*—and its readers—to look again at what Mr. Carter said and what his film stands for.

Let's not tear down those trying to raise our voices. Let's talk, even when the talk gets hard.

Yours in truth and unity,

Oscar Micheaux

The letter wasn't long—just a few hundred words—but it carried the authority of a man who had fought his own battles in the film industry and come out the other side. Micheaux had a way of weaving clarity with conviction and it struck a chord.

His endorsement not only bolstered Seth's credibility but also positioned the *Chronicle* as a paper aligned with Harlem's most respected voices. For once, management had placed its bet on the right side. It didn't hurt that the paper was selling like hotcakes.

The momentum built fast. That afternoon, Micheaux's words were quoted in editorials and debated in barbershops, beauty parlors and church meetings. By morning, our phone lines were jammed.

One of the operators passed a note: "Seth Carter's crew just called. They're grateful we ran the letter. Said it's taking the heat off him."

Reporters whispered as they passed one another in the hallways. Colleagues stopped by my desk with nods of approval and murmured congratulations. They understood what had been at stake and the significance of this moment. Seth's voice had landed—clear, measured, powerful. He hadn't just responded. He'd claimed the story.

Over the next few days, letters to the editor poured in. Most stood with Seth. A few railed against him for "airing our dirty laundry." But the volume told its own story: this wasn't a flash of attention. Seth had sparked a conversation that wasn't going away.

Out on Harlem's streets and in its cafes, people were talking. The article, the film—both had caught fire. The tide was turning, sweeping the conversation away from scandal and back to what mattered.

For the first time in weeks, I felt hope. Seth's vision had broken through the noise. Micheaux's words had reminded the *Chronicle*—and Harlem—of its greater purpose. Together, he and Seth had steered the conversation back to where it belonged: on the power of truth and the art of storytelling.

That morning, Selena Troy sat at her desk, eyes locked on the paper. By midday, the newsroom buzz had turned electric. Phones still rang. Voices carried. But Selena hadn't moved. She didn't turn the page. Didn't look up.

Quiet. The kind that draws a line around itself.

"Lanie."

I looked up to see Sam standing in his office doorway. He was holding a copy of the *Chronicle* like it was evidence in a trial.

"Got a minute?"

I followed him inside and shut the door. He leaned back against the desk, paper dangling from one hand.

"I'm not going to ask if you had anything to do with Seth showing up here. Or with Micheaux's letter."

I crossed my arms. "No?"

"Don't have to." He held up the front page. "Your finger-prints are all over it. Seth Carter doesn't decide to talk to us and Oscar Micheaux doesn't just happen to send in a letter that matched Carter's message point for point. One or the other, maybe. But not both. Not like this."

I said nothing.

Sam's mouth twitched. "Whatever you did, it worked. This paper hasn't had this much buzz in years. And more important—we're back on the right side of this story."

His eyes met mine. No bluff, no scold. Just the facts. "So, thank you. For steering us clear before we sank."

I shrugged. "Just doing my job."

He snorted. "With you, it's never just that."

I stepped in closer. Lowered my voice. "About Selena ..."

He paused. Nodded. "Yes. About her ..."

31

Twenty minutes later, I was back at my desk. The newsroom was quiet with all ears straining to hear what was going on in Sam's office.

I leaned back, making a show of reading my notes, but I couldn't help glancing at the glass. The others were the same—pretending to work, tapping away at their typewriters, ears cocked, waiting.

I sniffed the air, turned around. I swear, one guy had produced a bag of popcorn. I gave him a look. He shrugged and started chewing.

Sam hadn't drawn the blinds. That alone told us everything.

His office sat at the head of the walkway, like a command post, all windows. Usually, if there was trouble, he'd pull the blinds, keep it private. Not this time.

I couldn't hear them. Didn't need to.

Selena was fighting for her job—her career. I could tell that much. Her hands cut arcs through the air like she was trying to slice her way free. Probably claiming bad sources, a misunderstanding, maybe even sabotage.

But everyone knew the truth: quotes that didn't exist, scenes that never happened, stories stitched from threads too thin to hold. Wilkes had come forward, told Sam his story and confirmed the worst, providing damning evidence against her.

Sam didn't move. Just sat there, solid and still. No nods. No concessions. Arms crossed, leaning back just enough to make it clear: he was done giving her ground. And when she finally wound down, he gave her one sentence. Short. Deliberate.

This wasn't a warning—it was a judgment, delivered in full view.

I could guess what Sam was telling her. He was putting her back on the death beat. I could just hear him saying, "You can't be trusted to write responsibly about the living. Maybe, you'll do better with the dead."

The door to Sam's office flew open. It slammed against the wall with a bang that made half the room jump. Selena stormed out, her heels striking the floor like a firing squad's volley. She was halfway to her desk when she stopped. Turned. Found me.

She stared. Arms stiff. Fingers twitching. Then she came for me. Snarling. Lips drawn back like she meant to bite. From a distance, her eyes were cold, sharp. Up close, I saw something else—the glimmer of moisture. Tears? She blinked hard, like she could will them away. Like she knew she couldn't afford to cry in front of me.

"Congratulations," she hissed. "I hope you enjoy this."

I met her gaze. "Enjoy what, Selena?"

"Don't play coy. You've won this round. But one day it'll be your turn. Eventually, every spotlight burns."

The slap came before I knew what I'd moved.

A crack like a starter's pistol. Selena gasped. Her hand flew to her cheek. My palm stung, blood hot under the skin.

I kept my voice low. "I'd say that was for Seth and his crew. But it was for me. For Sam. For everyone else in here, too."

She turned slowly. Her gaze swept the room and I knew she saw what I saw—every eye on her, every jaw set tight. The quiet wasn't passive. It was loaded, ready to go off.

Then someone at the city desk clapped. One sharp mack of palm to palm. Another joined in. Then another.

Before long, the room was applauding, the claps crisp and measured. No cheer. Not even approval. Just release.

Selena spun on her heels, snatched her purse from her desk and stalked out. The door slammed so hard the glass rattled in its frame.

The clapping stopped. The room exhaled and silence rushed in.

Someone muttered, "Good riddance." A few nods. A few echoes.

Then the typewriters started again—soft at first, then rising, one key at a time. A chair creaked. A throat cleared.

Then it came back all at once.

Phones rang. Voices rose. Chairs scraped and rolled. Pages tore off copy spindles. The pit woke up and shook itself free.

A match struck. The hiss of sulfur. Somewhere down the row, a copyboy's shoes slapped the floor—quick, flat. Someone shouted across the room about a quote from DuBois. No answer. Just the clack-clack-ping of an Underwood coming up to speed. Drawers slammed. Papers flapped. Heat clanged through the pipes.

The pressroom door swung wide. A proof tray hit a desk. Thwack. Ink-smudged fingers left it behind without a word.

The sound hit me in the chest—solid, alive. It wasn't until then I realized how much Selena's presence had muted it, how the tension and resentment she generated had dampened it.

Over the years, I'd thought the noise would drive me out of my mind. But now I blessed it. That cacophony of phones, typewriter bells, voices reading copy, a pencil rolling off a desk and spinning on the floor. The newsroom wasn't just working again. It was breathing. It was set free.

And now it could once again roar.

I turned back to my notes. Selena was gone, with the smell of smoke still clinging to her heels. Her departure was satisfying but I didn't have time to dwell on it.

Somewhere out there, the truth about the sabotage was waiting to be uncovered. That's the story I had to tell.

My thoughts turned to Westbrook. The way he blinked at the light. The way he held that financial agreement inches from his face, like he couldn't quite bring it into focus.

Maybe it was nothing. Or maybe it was the reason he'd sunk his savings into Seth's film. Not just belief in the project, but desperation.

Despite all Westie's preaching about believing in Seth, I had to wonder—was he hedging his bets? Was he behind the sabotage?

A man losing his sight might do a lot of things to make sure he didn't go out broke. Or forgotten.

32

I t was early morning when I got the call. Something had happened on the movie set. Something terrible.

The sun hadn't fully risen, but the flashing red and blue lights painted the quiet Bronx street in harsh, stuttering colors. A knot of onlookers had formed in front of the entrance to the film set, with a few cops holding them back. As I shouldered my way through, I caught a glimpse of a familiar figure—that plain woman I'd seen with Westbrook, standing apart from the others, her face drawn with grief. But I barely registered her then, too focused on flashing my press pass at the uniformed officers to slip inside."

The set was a world away from the usual bustle. I'd never seen it so still. Cast and crew stood around, huddled in small, whispering clusters. Some were red-eyed, their faces smeared with make-up streaked by tears; others looked like ghosts, pale with shock. Some were whispering to one another, others weeping, some talking officers who were taking notes.

Seth was nowhere in sight.

In the center, beneath the harsh glare of the lights, a

makeshift rig had been constructed—planks and scaf-
folding rising up toward the shadows of the catwalks. A
crime scene photographer was perched on the wooden rig,
working a camera. At first, I couldn't see what he was snap-
ping pictures of. But then he moved and I saw the subject of
his focus: a man, suspended high up in mid-air.

A wide-shouldered man, built like a bulldozer.

Westbrook.

His body hung limp from the catwalk, swaying gently in
the draft that swept through the old stage. A thick coil of
rope twisted around his neck. It glowed white in the flood-
lights, sharp against the shadows around him. Reminded
me of a boa constrictor, one of those snakes that'll squeeze a
man to death, choke the living breath out of him.

A man dead. A death as unnatural as you can get. And, if
by suicide, the kind of death that some say damns a soul
forever. Happening on the set of a film called *Soul
Redemption*.

How ironic.

And tragic. For Westbrook. For Seth. And Clay. And
Grace. For the whole damn lot of them.

The rope looped through the fly system and strained
against a batten, creaking with each shift of weight. The
beams above seemed to groan under the burden. The coun-
terweights dangled beside him, as if mocking the man who
had once managed every inch of this space.

"You! Hey, you!"

I turned to see a short, stocky man with a trim mustache
marching toward me. He wore the New York detective's
favorite uniform: a cheap dark suit he didn't care about and
even cheaper black shoes dusty from pounding the streets. I
didn't know him, but I had a feeling he thought he knew me.
It was in his eyes. He'd heard stories. Not all of them good.

"Lanie Price." I extended my hand. "I'm—"

"I know who you are." He ignored my hand. "Heard about you from John Blackie."

That explained it. Blackie was NYPD Homicide, stationed at the Three-Two on West 135th Street, just across from my newspaper office. He and I had worked a number of cases together—me asking questions, him shutting doors.

"Blackie says you're a pest." Eyebrows raised, he sized me up for himself and I braced for an argument over whether I had a right to be there.

But then he did something cops rarely do. Surprised me. He gave a quick nod, decision made. "Gotta say, you don't look like much. But Blackie says you're okay. That you can even be useful now and then, 'specially when it comes to colored cases like this."

Colored cases?

I heard it. He meant me to. I didn't blink. Didn't give him the satisfaction. Blackie would never say that—and we both knew it.

I inclined my head. "And you are ...?"

"Arnold. Detective Montrose Arnold." Small, dark eyes. Pebbles pushed into a mottled pie of a face.

"Funny. He never mentioned you." I gave him a slow once-over, then shrugged. "Well, lucky for you, I'm useful on every kind of case."

"Is that so? I heard you like to make a mountain out of a mole hill. Well, today, you're outta luck." He jerked his meaty chin toward at Westbrook. "It's a clear case of suicide. Open and shut."

"You're sure about that?"

"Very sure. Cases like this? I seen it a thousand times. Apparently, he and the director got into it yesterday evening. Right here on set. Everybody heard it. The director accuses this guy of sabotage—breaking equipment, causing accidents, stuff that coulda killed someone. Fires him. Tells him not to run, says he's reporting him to the police. Then this guy here—"

"Westbrook."

"Yeah. Him. Comes back late last night and does himself in. Simple. Got caught. Didn't wanna face the heat. And did it here outta spite. Like I said, open and shut."

It was a reasonable conclusion—if you'd never known Westbrook. But I had. And I couldn't see it. Westie slipping back after hours, rigging the rope? Hands that had managed lights and lenses for four decades, now setting them up for his own last shot? Hmm-hmph. A tough old buzzard like him? Choosing to go out this way? No way.

"Who found him?"

"The director. First thing this morning. We got his statement already. He's in his office—with his brother. We're talking to the rest now—the cast, the crew."

Above us, the photographer called down, his voice echoing through the space. "All done. Tell the guys they can come and get him."

Arnold waved a hand. The cops moved in, began the slow process of lowering the body. The rope creaked as it slipped through the rigging. Beams above gave a low groan.

The air thickened—hard to breathe. Like wool.

A hush fell over the set. Respectful. Heavy. The body drifted down, sometimes with a jerk, the rope creaking in the silence. Even the lights seemed to hold their breath, waiting for something unnamed.

When the body finally touched the ground, the stillness deepened. Police chatter rose again, soft and routine, as they got back to work.

One of the cops flicked open a jackknife, hacked

through the rope. The part still looped around Westbrook's neck flopped down like a decapitated but stubborn snake, refusing to let go. They heaved the remains onto the gurney and started to cover him with a sheet.

"Hold on," Arnold said.

He strode over to take a closer look. So did I.

Arnold glanced back, gave me the eye. A silent *stay in your lane.*

I didn't flinch. "You don't expect me to stand behind the line like a schoolgirl, do you? I can't see a thing from over there."

He looked at me for a long second. "You're not going to go away, are you?"

I shook my head once.

He closed his eyes, took a deep breath and blew it out through puffed cheeks. "Okay. Fine. You think you can handle the sight of this stiff? Be my guest."

He made a sweeping gesture toward the body, then took a theatrical step aside. "Like Blackie said. What Miss Lanie wants, Miss Lanie gets."

Flat on his back, still and ashen, Westbrook looked less like a man of flesh and blood than a marionette made of wood. His eyes and mouth were closed. The muscles of his face hung loose. There were no signs he'd clawed at the rope, no bruises on his hands or marks on his neck. Nothing to show he'd tried to get free, fought for breath.

But there was a wound—a gash on the right side of his head, near the temple. And a thin line of dried blood trailed down the side of his face, not along the cheekbone, but down toward the ear.

I pointed to it. "Look at that. That's not from the rope."

Arnold bent, took a closer look. Scratched his chin. Shrugged like it cost him something. "Maybe he banged his head when he jumped. Happens. Could've knocked him out cold. Went out easy."

I didn't move. Just kept looking at him. What a stellar piece of deductive work. "You ever seen blood flow uphill, Detective?"

His eyes narrowed. The edge crept in. "Don't try to be cute, Price. It's a suicide. End of story. You see enough of these, you know what you're looking at."

I stayed quiet. Pretended I didn't hear him.

But doubt crept in.

Was I was reading too much into it? Maybe it was just what it seemed—a desperate man, backed into a corner, taking the only way out he saw. Maybe I'd seen too many crime scenes. Read too much Chandler, Hammett, Christie. Maybe I was seeing shadows.

But then my gaze drifted back—to that blood, dried and dark, pooled in the cup of his ear.

The path it followed didn't match Arnold's story.

And just like that, the doubt burned off—like mist in early sun.

Arnold might've thought he had this case wrapped up— but he was missing the obvious.

A wound that wasn't an accident.

A death that wasn't suicide.

And a setup meant to cloak murder.

33

I left Arnold to it and headed to Seth's office. Found him slumped in his chair, phone to his ear. Clay leaned against Seth's desk, arms folded tight across his chest. They looked up when I walked in. Seth muttered something into the receiver, then hung up.

"Lanie." He managed a weak smile and gestured to a chair. "I thought you might stop by. Take a seat."

Script pages littered the desk. There was a half-full coffee cup that looked like it had gone cold hours ago.

"How're you doing?" I asked them both. Clay answered.

"We've been better."

"I can imagine." They looked ragged. "Where's Grace?"

"She's on her way," Seth said.

His eyes were sunken, the circles darker, the lines on his face deeper since the last time I'd seen him.

"That detective tells me you were the one who found him. What happened?"

Clay shot me a worried look. "Seth, you don't have to answer—"

Seth held his hand up. "It's fine. Maybe... maybe, she should know."

Seth drew a hand down his face. "It's been... God, it's been a mess. We thought we had everything lined up. But a few days ago, we started having equipment trouble. It was always the cameras—cables coming loose, lights cutting out. Even had a lens shatter on us in the middle of a shot. Each time, Westbrook was the last one to touch the gear."

Clay chimed in. "We figured it was him. Who else? He's been griping about the production for weeks—about Seth's 'artsy' shots, the tight deadlines. Said the whole thing would fall apart and he wasn't quiet about it."

Seth nodded, his shoulders sagging. "Last night, I confronted him. He didn't deny it. Just gave me this strange look and said, 'You think you know everything, don't you, kid?' I lost it. Told him to get off the set. That I'd report him. I didn't mean it. I was angry. I said whatever came to mind. I never thought ... I never thought he'd do this."

He rubbed his face again, let out a shuddering breath. Clay laid a hand on Seth's shoulder, as if to comfort him, but the gesture seemed awkward, hollow.

"I shouldn't have pushed him so hard," Seth said. "I thought I could scare him into admitting what he'd done, but..."

"But now he's gone," Clay finished. "And he brought it on himself."

"Don't say that." Seth massaged his forehead. "I just ... I just didn't think he'd do something like this."

"So, you think it's suicide, too," I said.

They both looked up fast.

"What else could it be?" Clay asked. "Maybe you didn't see—maybe they'd taken him down by the time you got here, but—"

"No, I saw. And I talked to that cop, Arnold. He's sure it's suicide."

"But you're not." Seth straightened up. "But that ... that would mean—"

"Aww. She's just giving you the bunk." Clay gave me a warning look. "That cop's the expert. If he says it was a suicide, then it's suicide."

Seth looked from Clay to me. "Lanie?"

Clay's gaze stayed on me. "I know you mean well, Miss Lanie. But now's not the time to be stirring up trouble. We got enough as it is. Seth's been on the phone with investors all morning. They're ready to pull out again. Suicide's bad enough, but if you start rumors that it was—"

"I don't trade in rumors," I said. "I write facts. Or I write nothing. That's what I did here. Remember? I held the story. And now I wonder if I was wrong. If a man would still be alive if I hadn't."

Clay looked like he'd bitten into a sour apple. "So what are you going to do?"

"Write it up."

"Putting your own slant on it?"

"I'll quote the cops, if that makes you feel better."

"It doesn't," Seth said. "A man's dead and I drove him to it. I thought I was protecting my people. Instead..." He shook his head. "I've ruined the production. For everybody." With a dark chuckle, he added, *"Soul Redemption.* The production from hell."

For a moment, no one said anything. Then I stood up.

"Seth, mind if I took a look around? Might be my only chance before everything gets cleaned up."

Clay stiffened and I could see the protest rising in his throat. "That's not a good idea. What do you think you're going to find?"

"Don't know. But I've learned to trust my instincts."

"Then let me go with you."

I shook my head. "Thanks, but I can manage."

Seth glanced between us, then waved me on. "Go ahead. Just be careful."

He looked at Clay. "Besides, I need you here. Everyone else is off for the day. But they're supposed to be back tomorrow. God only knows how many will show up. Meanwhile, we've got to revise the schedule—one of the angels has already pulled out and there could be a few more. That means less money and less time."

Clay hesitated.

"Come on," Seth said. "Let her do her thing and we'll do ours."

Clay didn't look convinced. "Fine. Just... be careful up there, alright? Last thing we need is another accident."

"Understood." I walked out.

Two brothers, same blood, different hearts. Seth drowning in guilt, Clay busy building walls. Made me wonder which one had more to hide.

34

The catwalk loomed above like a skeleton in the rafters, crisscrossing the ceiling in long, narrow lines of iron. I left my purse on a crate backstage and approached the access ladder. Not the kind painters use with flat steps. This one had rounded metal rungs, like you'd see on ships. Built for narrow, vertical climbs.

I stood there for a minute, staring up and wondering how I'd let curiosity get ahead of common sense. I was scared of heights, always had been. What the heck was I thinking?

Well, there was nothing for it now. A man was dead and I needed to find out why. I rubbed my sweaty palms on my dress, slipped off my heels and set my foot on the lowest rung.

It wasn't too bad at first—the ladder held steady. But the higher I got, the more it wobbled and the harder my heart thumped. Halfway up, my heart beat so hard the blood pounded in my ears. Every breath clawed its way out. The air felt cooler up here. Thinner. A musty smell of old dust and metal hung in the space, undisturbed for months.

Above me, ropes and cables twisted in a complex web. Shadows stretched like fingers across the darkened set. The catwalk seemed endlessly far away. By the time I reached it, I was in a cold sweat. I heaved myself over the edge and sat there, catching my breath—trying not to look down.

I got to my feet but crouched low and edged along the walkway. The iron framework seemed solid enough, but the flooring was patched with old wooden planks, faded and worn. Each step made it creak. From below, the empty set looked like a doll's house, voices from stagehands distant and small.

The rope that had held Westbrook still dangled from the support beam, swaying with the draft that whispered across my neck. I forced myself to look over the edge, down to where he'd fallen. My stomach dropped. Dizziness hit in a wave. I swallowed hard, steadying myself before straightening up. Then I turned to the catwalk itself.

That's when I saw it—wedged against the rail, glinting in the pale light filtering from above. A short length of pipe, not more than a foot long. Something dark and crusted stained one end.

I pulled a handkerchief from my pocket, wrapped it around the pipe and lifted it. Heavier than it looked. As I turned it, gray nappy curls caught the light. Westbrook's? Had to be.

No accident. And sure as hell not suicide.

Metal creaked behind me. I whipped around, heart jumping. The pipe became a weapon in my grip. A shadow loomed twenty feet away, large and shapeless in the dim light. For a heartbeat, I couldn't breathe. The figure emerged from the shadows—Seth, his face pale, eyes fixed on me.

Relief washed over me. "You scared the hell out of me."

My voice came out sharp. "What are you doing up here? Thought you'd be going over the script with Clay."

"I... I couldn't focus." He ran a hand over his slicked hair. "All I keep thinking about is what happened, what I should have done differently." He stepped forward. The catwalk trembled slightly. "Then I started worrying about you. Clay was right. I shouldn't have let you come up here alone." His gaze dropped to the pipe in my hands. "What's that?"

My first impulse was to lie, but why bother? The pipe's rough weight pressed into my palm through the handkerchief. I unwrapped it and held it up between us.

"Found this wedged up here. I think it's what hit Westbrook before he went over."

Seth went still. His face drained of color. He stared at the pipe like it was something out of his worst nightmare.

"There's blood on it," I said. "And hair. I'm going to take it to the police, see if they can match it."

He let out a shallow breath. "Lanie, think about this. What you're suggesting—you're talking about murder." His voice dropped lower as he took another step forward. The metal framework groaned. "Do you know what that could do to the film? To everyone involved?"

"Better to know the truth than live with a lie." It sounded self-righteous, even to my ears. Maybe callous. But it was what I believed.

He moved closer, the space between us narrowing to ten feet. His voice turned soft, almost pleading. "What if you're wrong? Suspicions like that take on a life of their own. They never die." He rubbed his temples, exhaustion etched in every line of his face. "You'll just hurt people. Clay, the crew —me."

His hand dropped to his side, then rose toward me. His fingers curled. "I already have enough on my shoulders.

Don't make this harder." His voice hardened. "Now, give it here."

That shift—from nearly begging to demanding. The way his hand stretched toward me. My pulse quickened. I took a half-step back, the pipe tight in my grip.

A terrifying thought flashed through my mind: What if it was Seth? What if all this pressure—the film, the finances, his cast and crew—had finally made him snap?

I searched his face for reassurance. Found only strain and desperation. The pipe in my hand matched the mark on Westbrook's head like a key to a lock. "I can't just walk away, Seth. I owe it to Westbrook to find out what happened."

His eyes narrowed, incredulous. "You owe it to Westbrook? That man sabotaged us, nearly brought everything crashing down." He took another step. Only six feet between us now. "What do you mean you '*owe*' him? If you owe anybody, it's the living, not the dead. The people who've been working like dogs, day and night, to make this film happen." His voice rose. "If you call Westbrook's death murder, you'll do as much damage as he did—no, more. You'll kill this film as sure as—"

His voice caught. His mouth clamped shut.

I took a steadying breath, feeling a chill along my spine. "As surely as what, Seth?"

A terrible silence. The catwalk seemed to sway though neither of us moved. Was he about to confess? Was he the one who'd sent Westbrook over the edge?

Their fight had been public. What happened afterward wasn't. We just had Seth's word that he'd found the body when he came in early. Westbrook had supposedly left the set after their fight. But then why come back? Arnold figured it was to kill himself—to avoid prosecution or make one last defiant gesture against Seth.

But what if it was to meet someone? Meet Seth?

Seth took another step forward, the catwalk giving a metallic sigh. His hand remained outstretched, his mouth set. Something dark flashed in his eyes.

I took a step back. My foot hit a rotten board. The wood splintered with a sharp crack. My foot twisted, the world tilted and I stumbled backward. Arms flailing, I tipped sideways over the edge.

Seth lunged forward—grabbed me by the shoulders. Panic flared, sharp and wild. I swung the pipe at him. The blow grazed his arm. He didn't let go.

"Lanie!" He yanked me back, steadying me as I regained my footing.

I shook him off, breathless, chest heaving as the pipe dangled from my hand. He stood there, silent, watching me with hurt and frustration.

I wanted to believe he'd saved me by instinct. That he was only there to help. But I couldn't forget that darkness in his eyes. Couldn't shake the feeling I was looking at a man on a razor's edge—someone who might've reached out to save me but was just as capable of letting go.

He seemed to read something in my face and turned away. Leaned on the railing. Rubbed his hands together, looked down at them, flexed them. Stared out over the empty set below.

When he spoke again, his voice was hollow. "Do what you have to do. But remember—sometimes, the truth costs more than it's worth."

35

It was mid-morning when I got to the newsroom. A few of the others raised an eyebrow at the sight of me. They knew it was usually well after noon before I rolled in.

Not today.

Sam's door stood open, blinds half-drawn. He was at his desk, sleeves rolled, fingers pressed to his temple like he was holding something in.

I rapped the doorframe. "Got a minute?"

He looked up. "Lanie. Yeah. You finish checking out the Westbrook story?"

I stepped in, closed the door behind me. "Just came back from there."

"They're saying Westbrook took his own life."

I eased into the chair across from him. "That's what they're saying, yes."

He went still. Looked at me. "But you don't believe it."

"No."

He drew a deep breath, let it out. His expression said it all.

Here we go again.

I waited for the reprimand. It didn't come. Just that quiet understanding between two people who've already walked through fire together.

"What makes you think it wasn't suicide?"

Funny how so many people can't bring themselves to say the word. *Murder.*

"I saw the body. Up close. He had a head wound. One the fall didn't explain."

I reached into my bag and pulled out the handkerchief-wrapped pipe. Unrolled it on his desk like a weapon tossed on the table between outlaws.

"I climbed up on catwalk. Found this."

Sam stared at it. Didn't touch it.

"Blood and hair," I said. "Matches the wound. Someone used it."

Still, he didn't move. "So Westbrook didn't jump."

"No. Someone helped him over."

He nodded slowly, drawing his hand down over his face. "Which means murder. Which means ... " He thought it over. "You talked to the cops?"

"Caught the detective on the scene. He was not happy to see me."

Sam gave a dry little snort. "Reputation precedes you, huh."

"Something like that. Doesn't matter. He's already made up his mind. Suicide. Open-and-shut."

"This all the proof you've got?"

"For now."

Another nod.

"Any idea who did it?"

I thought about that bad moment with Seth up on the catwalk. The look in his eyes. The desperation that hadn't landed.

"No."

Sam leaned back, arms crossed. His gaze never left the pipe.

"They'll say you're stirring up trouble again."

"They always do."

"And you'll do it anyway."

"You know me."

He didn't smile.

"The story of Westbrook's death is bigger than the sabotage piece. Are you ready to write it clean? No hedging. No protecting Seth this time."

"I'm ready."

"No guesses in print. Nothing you can't prove."

"I know. I won't."

"But the rest."

"Like I said. I won't hold back this time."

There was a certain irony here. Before he was worried about me not saying enough. Now he was worried I'd say too much.

He looked at me a long moment. And then said, flatly: "You know what would make management happy?"

"I can imagine. A nice little package of a story, one that blames the sabotage on Westie and has him kill himself. Done and dusted. No more scandal. No more nothing."

"You give them that, they'll love you forever."

"I'm not giving them a lie."

"Then you'd better have the facts. Because these days? Truth's not good enough."

[A BEAT]

"Your little plan to save Seth? Worked too well. He's gone from problem child to golden boy. And now we can't lay a finger on him. I'm not saying he had anything to do with it, but even if he did—we'd have to be mighty careful about saying it."

"Management doesn't care about protecting Seth. They just care about protecting themselves."

"Damn straight they do."

[A BEAT]

He didn't say the rest. That he thought he could finally take a breath. *Exhale.* Selena was gone. The dust was settling.

He and I—we weren't where we had been and there was no telling we ever would be, but for a few hours there, things had been better.

He didn't say it, but I heard it anyway: *I thought the worst was over.*

Now here I was, bucking the system, dragging him into it. He was caught between me and management, again.

"Sam, I didn't plan it this way."

"No. You never do.

His tone wasn't cruel. Just tired.

"Lanie, we've got to be smart about this. Selena kept us busy. Too busy to think about the saboteur. But he's been out there the whole time. And now he's struck again."

"I think Westbrook got too close."

"And if you do the same?"

"I play it right, he won't know I'm close until it's too late."

"No, Lanie. No." He shook his head, a man done arguing. "Just take the damn pipe to the cops. Let them do their job. Let it be.

"You know I can't do that."

He let out a long, slow breath. "Yeah. I know."

"I'm going to find out what Westbrook knew. And finish the story he started."

Sam stared at the pipe like it might start bleeding on its own. Then he looked at me. That look he gets when he's torn between backing me and bolting the newsroom door shut.

"I can barely protect you in here. I sure as hell can't protect you out there."

I don't expect you to. The words jumped to the tip of my tongue, but I caught them. They would've only hurt him. And they were a lie—a lie I told myself so I could keep going.

"I know, Sam. It's okay. I know."

I wrapped the pipe back in the handkerchief, slipped it into my bag and stood.

He didn't say anything else. Neither did I.

I turned for the door.

"Lanie."

I looked back. He wasn't looking at me—just at the papers scattered across his desk. One hand hand rested flat on the desk, palm down, steadying himself.

"Whatever you find," he said, "don't carry it alone."

36

I was back in the Bronx early the next morning, stepping into Detective Arnold's office, the pipe wrapped tightly in a handkerchief and clutched under my arm.

Given my experience with Blackie's clutter, I thought Arnold's office was surprisingly neat. Forms and files were stacked with precision on one side of his desk; file cabinets were lined up against the wall like soldiers at attention. This was a man who liked to be in control. But that did not necessarily mean he was thorough—that was left to be seen.

The detective himself sat behind a well-used desk, hunched over paperwork, his shoulder-strap cutting deep into his shoulder, his police issue firearm hanging heavily from it. He was aware of my presence—after all I'd only gotten in to see him after he'd told the desk sergeant to let me in, but he let me stand there, intentionally ignoring me for two long minutes. Finally, I cleared my throat.

"Detective."

"Price," he sighed. "I hoped—prayed—you'd have moved on."

I ignored the jab—and the rudeness—and laid the pipe

down on his desk, letting the handkerchief unfold to show the dark stains and the gray curls that had stuck to the rough metal. "I found this up on the catwalk. It was wedged against the railing—"

He raised an eyebrow but made no move to touch it. "And?"

"And," I said, drawing out the word, "I think this is what hit Westbrook. Matches the wound on his temple. The hair on it? Could be his." I pointed to the faint stain on the fabric. "I'm willing to bet that if you tested it, you'd find his blood, too."

Arnold pinched the bridge of his nose as if I were a migraine he couldn't shake. "So what?" He shrugged. "It's a theater set. Tools get left around all the time. That doesn't make this," he gestured dismissively to the pipe, "some kind of smoking gun. And as for Westbrook, he was a washed-up bitter old man. Drunk half the time—"

"I never saw him drunk—"

"And apparently sabotaging that movie the rest of the time. You think I'm gonna spin my wheels over some rusted piece of pipe?"

His attitude didn't surprise me—I'd half expected as much—but that didn't make it any easier to swallow. I took a deep breath.

"This wasn't an accident. The way I see it, someone knocked him out with this, then strung him up to make it look like suicide. He agreed to meet someone on that set and that person killed him."

Arnold sighed and shook his head. He threw down his pen. "Blackie warned me. God only knows why he doesn't reign you in. But he's not me. And you're not in his precinct district. You're in mine. And I won't have you raising dust and causing havoc."

If I'd had time to think about it, it I might've felt hurt that Blackie had 'warned' him against me. Then again, I'm not sure I would've believed Arnold, anyway. Either way, I just plowed ahead, pointing to the pipe. "*This here* is *evidence* that Westbrook didn't just fall. He was hit. This pipe could be the murder weapon. Look at the hair on it. Look at the blood—"

"Do you know how many people have been up on that catwalk?" He shook his head, picking up the pipe and holding it as if it were a child's forgotten toy. "You're reading too much into it. You found some junk on a stage. That's all."

"It's not junk. Westbrook had a very specific wound on his temple, right where this could've hit him."

I finished, hoping against hope that he'd crack, give me something. But he rolled his eyes and pushed the pipe back toward me with a flick of his fingers. "You're always trying to make a mountain out of a molehill, Price. Maybe Blackie lets you get away with it. But I won't—not in my precinct."

"Detective—"

"No," he snapped, cutting me off. "This isn't one of your little newspaper stories where you can bend the facts to fit your narrative. This is real police work and I don't have the time or patience for theories based on half-baked hunches." He gestured to the pipe with a scoff. "Take this junk home and leave the real work to us."

I forced myself to stay calm. "Look, I'm just asking you to look into it. Isn't that your job? There's a dead man and his death doesn't add up."

Arnold gave me that same flat, condescending stare he'd worn since I walked in. The kind of look that said he'd made up his mind and nothing short of an earthquake would change it.

"My job," he said, "is to separate fact from fantasy. This," he gestured to the pipe again, "is fantasy. And I'm done letting you waste my time. Take this junk home and leave the real work to the professionals."

Frustration roiled inside but I kept my expression steady. "Fine. But don't say I didn't warn you. If Westbrook was murdered, someone's walking around free because you chose not to look."

He waved a dismissive hand, already turning back to his paperwork. "Close the door on your way out."

I pressed my lips together to keep from saying what I wanted to say, grabbed up the pipe and left his office. Clearly, if I was going to prove Westbrook was murdered, I'd have to do it without the police.

37

No one said Westbrook's name, but his absence was the loudest thing on set.

And I was there to tell the story. To drum up a soft sob piece about how the production was coping, how things were just ticking along—or not.

But I had my own reasons for being there. I wasn't just there to listen. I meant to catch the cracks between reality and make-believe—or whatever bald-faced lies folks were ready to feed me.

Not an easy proposition on a film set, where lying's not just tolerated—it's paid for.

But I was never one to give up easily. Especially in a case like this. A man like Sydney Westbrook doesn't check out early. Someone punched his ticket. And I intended to find out who stamped it.

Seth had pretty much given me free rein on the set. I was standing near the main lighting rig, flipping through my notes, when I caught the murmur of voices nearby.

"Strangest thing," one guy was saying. "Didn't think the old man had it in him."

"You sure it was him?" another asked.

"Swear on my mother. Saw him more than once, slipping into that hotel during lunch breaks and sometimes right after work. You know the one,—the Emerson—about a block away."

"You think he had a sheba over there?"

"Didn't think so, but now ... well, now, yeah, I do."

"An old broke nigga like him?"

"Man, that nigga weren't broke. He was close with his cash. I'm sure he had a pile stashed away. Anyway, you know what they say. Just 'cause there's snow on the roof don't mean there's no fire in the belly—or something like that."

A pause. Someone shifted, scuffing a boot against the concrete floor. "You think that's why he did it? That he got involved with a working woman and she took all his cash away?"

A nervous chuckle. "Wouldn't be the first time."

A third voice: "You really think Westie offed himself over a woman?"

That first voice: "It'd make more sense than him just hanging himself out of the blue."

They moved away, leaving me in thought. It was a startling idea, that Westie might've killed himself over a woman.

Startling, but wrong. It didn't add up. Not to me.

A flicker of memory—the woman in the crowd outside the police line, her face pale, stricken. She hadn't been gawking like the rest, hadn't been whispering theories to the person next to her. She had been watching, waiting.

Maybe Westbrook had been meeting someone at a hotel. Maybe there was something to what they were saying. But if he was sneaking off, it wasn't for romance. Not a man like that. It was for something else. Something he couldn't put on a call sheet.

And I meant to find out what.

38

The lobby felt like it belonged to another time, the kind of place where footsteps softened on worn rugs and the air held the faint scent of old wood and lemon polish. A fan turned lazily above the reception desk, stirring the warm air without cooling it.

Behind the counter, a woman arranged a stack of receipts, her movements precise but mechanical, as though going through the motions kept her upright. I recognized her face the moment I stepped inside.

"Excuse me." I stepped forward. "I think we've seen each other before."

She glanced up, her eyes narrowing slightly. "Sorry, but I don't—"

"It was on the movie set. You were with Sydney Westbrook."

Her fingers stilled for just a moment before resuming. "You must be mistaken."

"No, you were there. And later, that day, when the police came, you were in the crowd outside the set."

She stacked the papers, aligning their edges with unnecessary precision. "A lot of people were there."

"You looked upset."

Her shoulders rose in a stiff shrug. "What can I say? It was upsetting."

I put my purse down and leaned on the counter. "You knew him, didn't you? Sydney Westbrook. You knew him personally."

She paused, her grip tightening on the stack of papers. "All right. Yes, I knew him. Why? What's it any business of yours?"

"I'd like to understand what happened to him."

"He died. That's what happened."

"It wasn't that simple and we both know it."

"What does that mean?"

"It means a man like him doesn't just up and kill himself."

Her eyes widened and I could sense her shock, but I wasn't sure what was behind it. Had I pushed too hard, too fast? Maybe she didn't agree. Or maybe she did and the idea of someone else seeing it, too, left her shaken. I couldn't tell which. Her next words gave me my answer.

"Why would you care?"

Now I could see her reaction for what it was. There was shock, yes, but there was also recognition, as if I'd spoken a truth she hadn't dared to say aloud.

"I care because I do," I said. "Sydney Westbrook was a good man. He lived a life worth honoring and he died a death worth investigating."

I thought I was making progress, that my sincere remarks would help me gain her trust. But I was wrong.

Her expression hardened. "Look, sister, I know all about you. You and that paper of yours. All y'all care about is making noise, making money. Y'all wrote all them mean things about the movie Sydney was working on. Stirred up a lot of trouble for him and his people."

"I didn't write those articles."

"Doesn't matter. Your paper did."

"I'm not here for them. I'm here for him."

She studied me for a long moment, then turned away, her shoulders slumped. "People always want to ask questions after it's too late."

"That doesn't mean the answers aren't worth finding."

She said nothing, but I saw how her hands trembled before she clasped them together. I saw how she pressed her eyes closed for a moment and gave her head a little shake. Then she faced me again and her eyes, now soft with unshed tears, searched mine, seeking a reason to trust me. I guess she found one because she finally gave a curt nod and said, "Come on," then led me to a small sitting area by the windows.

39

We sat across from each other, separated by a low table scuffed with years of use. She rested her hands in her lap, fingers twisting together.

"Sydney was ... important to me," she began. "We were important to each other."

She stopped there. Glanced down. Her fingers kept working, slow and nervous.

"I never expected anything. Been here too long for that kind of foolishness. But there was something about him. That first day, he came in asking about a couple. Normally, I don't say a word. Learned the hard way to keep my mouth shut. But Sydney ... he had a way about him. Made you want to trust him."

Her hands stilled. For a moment, I thought she wouldn't go on.

"He kept coming back," she said finally. "At first, it was about the film, sure. But soon it wasn't. He started asking about me. My day. Whether I liked working here. Said the front desk suited me. Called it a 'command post' like I was keeping the world running from behind that counter."

A faint smile. "It wasn't anything grand. No declarations. Just little talks. The kind that sneak up on you. He'd tell me about the films he'd worked on, the cities he'd passed through. Places I'd never see. He made them sound like adventures, even the lonely ones. And when I talked ... he listened."

She looked at me then. Straight on.

"Not many people listen when you work behind a desk like mine. He did. Made me feel ..."

She didn't finish the thought. She didn't have to.

Her fingers gripped together tighter. "He told me once he didn't know what came next. Said he'd spent so long working, he didn't know how to stop. But then he smiled, touched my hand and said maybe he was starting to figure it out."

That smile was gone now. The stillness that replaced it was heavy.

"We didn't need to spell it out. It was just there. We both knew."

She looked away. Swallowed. "And now it's gone. Everything we thought might've been. Our chance. It's gone."

She drew a deep breath. Blinked hard.

"We were going to get lunch. One real lunch. Not coffee in the lobby. Not a countertop hello. A real moment, away from all of this." Her voice thickened. "That was the day he died."

The words landed with a soft thud. Like something closing. Her hands fell still in her lap.

"I keep wondering. Why? He was happy. He was looking forward to seeing me. There was no sign—of anything. Or was there? Did I miss it?"

I opened my mouth. Closed it.

Sadie's voice was quieter now. Smaller.

"They say it was suicide. That he put a piece of rope around his neck and jumped. But I don't know. I can't make it make sense. Not after what he said. Not after how he looked at me. And if it wasn't suicide—" she shook her head, eyes shining, "—then someone killed him. And I don't know which truth is worse."

I leaned forward slightly, but not too far. She was balancing on a thread. One breath in the wrong place, she'd retreat.

"You loved him."

She gave the faintest nod.

"That doesn't go away," I said. "Even when the story ends ugly."

Her eyes found mine. "No. It doesn't."

And for one brief moment, I saw it. The loneliness. The not knowing. The cruel weight of *almost.*

I carried my own.

40

S he didn't say anything else. Just rose and crossed to the window, like memory had wrung her out and left her empty.

She pulled a silver cigarette case from her pocket, tapped one out. "Got a match?"

I dug out a book of matches, tossed it to her. She caught it, lit up and inhaled deep. Through the window's wavy glass, the street shimmered like a mirage. Summer was cooking the pavement outside, but in here the fan kept turning, stirring memories instead of cooling them.

"You said Sydney first came here looking for a couple."

She blew smoke toward the ceiling. "Yes, a man and woman." Another drag, slower this time. "He described how they looked, dressed. Said they were causing trouble for someone he cared about." She turned from the window. "That he needed to know the truth."

"And you told him what you knew."

"He showed me their pictures. I told him they'd just left." She moved to a cabinet behind the front desk, came back with a bottle and two glasses. "Funny thing was, I had the feeling he already knew that. Like he'd been watching the place."

I could picture it—Westbrook waiting under the flickering streetlight, hat tilted low, watching. The thought settled like cold lead in my gut.

Sadie poured two fingers in each glass. "Then he wanted to see their room."

"Did you let him?"

She pushed a glass toward me, took a long sip from her own. "Shouldn't have. But there was something about Sydney. Made it hard to say no."

"He had that effect on people."

"Yes and he convinced me it was important. That he wasn't trying make trouble but prevent it."

A ghost of a smile touched her lips, faded fast. "So I took him upstairs." She took a swallow, set her glass down hard. "He searched the place. Dresser, closet. Got down on his hands and knees, felt under the bed." Her fingers tightened around her glass. "That's when he found it."

"Found what?"

"Something small. Fit right in his palm. Never showed it to me, but I saw his face when he pulled it out." She drained her glass. "Never saw anyone look like that before. Like whatever he found proved something he'd been praying wasn't true."

"Did he say anything about it?"

"Just that he'd seen a wrong that needed setting right." She walked back to the window, cigarette burning forgotten between her fingers."

"The couple, do they still come here?"

"No. The visits stopped—"

"When? After Sydney died?"

"Before that."

"How long before?"

She thought about it. "Right after he gave me the movie set tour."

"That was the day I met you?"

"The lights, the noise, the people. The whole place jumping like a live wire. It all fit him. He belonged there." She let out a quiet breath. "Wanted to show me his world, he said. But I think he was hoping I'd recognize something —and I did."

"You saw them, the couple?"

"Just her."

"The woman?"

"Took me a minute to recognize her without the get-up. No wig, no paint. Looking proper as Sunday." Sadie's laugh was dry as autumn leaves. "Funny how different people can look when they're not pretending."

"Did she notice you?"

"No. She was too busy to notice anything. Probably wouldn't have recognized me anyway. People like me, we're invisible. People look right through us."

Being invisible. She wasn't bitter about it. This was just the way it was in her world. It made me think of mine—how most of the people I knew, including reporters like Selena, spent every waking minute scheming to be noticed, clawing for the spotlight like their lives depended on it.

"Did Westbrook tell you who she was?"

"He didn't offer and I didn't ask. Some things, you're better off not knowing."

I couldn't disagree with her there. For some, knowledge is power. For others, it's deadly.

"What about the man?"

Sadie frowned. "Didn't see him. He wasn't there." She crushed out her cigarette.

"Do you think he was wearing a disguise when he came here?"

"Probably. His mustache was crooked half the time. I guess he didn't care—or didn't think he needed much of one."

I paused, reflecting. Finally: "What about the names they signed in under?"

She rattled them off and later showed me the register. The names meant nothing. Neither did the handwriting.

But none of that mattered. By then, I had a inkling as to who they were.

And why Westbrook ended up dead.

41

I left Sadie's hotel and stepped into a late-afternoon haze thick with exhaust and regret. The sun had dipped low, but the air hadn't cooled. A man whistled for a cab that never came. A woman dragged a cranky child across the street, each step a battle.

I kept walking.

Sadie's voice still rang in my ears. *He was looking forward to seeing me... There was no sign—of anything.* The pain of not knowing. The way it ate at her. The way it always would.

I'd told her that kind of love doesn't disappear, even when the story ends ugly.

But what I hadn't said—what I couldn't—was that I understood.

Not because of Westbrook. But because of Hamp.

Because I still didn't know what he'd carried in those last months. What fears he'd kept hidden. What truths he'd buried for my sake. And maybe that was easier—for him. Maybe silence was the only kindness he had left to give.

But it left me with ghosts. And questions. And guilt.

Sadie missed her moment. She'd found something real

and she never got the chance to live it. I was on the verge of doing the same. Sam had offered me a key, a life. I turned it down. Told myself I needed more time. But how much time did I really have?

Sometimes the door doesn't stay open.

And sometimes you don't get the chance to knock again.

I didn't know what I was going to say when I got there. I only knew I had to ask. I had to know the truth.

The heat lay heavy on Lenox Avenue, making the air shimmer over the blacktop. Even the shade under the awnings felt stale. I crossed the street, skirted a busted hydrant that was spilling a thin stream into the gutter and turned the corner.

The old sign came into view: Russell Free Clinic—hand-painted and peeling.

Nothing like the fresh, hopeful place Hamp had proudly shown me years ago. Back then, everything gleamed with promise.

Now it just looked beaten.

The two had met in medical school. After graduation, Hamp had gone back to Chicago, Lionel to New York, but they stayed in touch. Years later, both seasoned and restless, Lionel wrote Hamp to say he was giving up his prestige post at Harlem Hospital. Was Hamp interested? Hamp was.

They were thick as thieves from the moment we arrived. They talked about the clinic, about what it could be. It had been Lionel's dream, one of many and it became Hamp's too. Turned out to be the only dream Hamp had time to make real.

My husband had family money. He became one of the main backers. After he died, I avoided the clinic. Walked past it a hundred times and kept going. Told myself it brought back too many memories. But standing there now, looking at it from the outside, I knew better. It was guilt.

I took a deep breath, braced myself and went inside.

The waiting room hit me like a furnace. Windows cracked open. Fans buzzing uselessly. Bodies packed tight. Sweat and medicinal alcohol filled my nose. Exhausted mothers fanned crying babies with church bulletins. An old man dabbed his forehead with a handkerchief that had seen better days. A young fellow slumped in the corner, head in hands.

Cracked tiles. Battered chairs. Exposed pipes running along water-stained walls. This wasn't a clinic. It was a last stand against TB, hunger and cheap hooch. Outgunned and running low on ammunition.

It was clear Lionel hadn't found a way to replace the money Hamp had brought in. I wished I could have stepped in, but the truth was, I couldn't. The house and a modest allowance had come to me. But the family money—the real money—had stayed locked up in Chicago, right where it was always meant to.

A young woman stood behind the desk, sorting a stack of dog-eared files. Maybe a nurse. I was about to walk up and ask for Lionel when he entered from the back room. Despite the heat, he looked crisp. Reminded me of Hamp that way. Cool, no matter how high the temperature.

I used to tease him about it. He put up with it for a while, then he gave me an answer that shut my mouth.

"People deserve to feel they're being treated by a professional, Lanie. Even if—especially if—they're poor. They need to feel respected. That's all I'm doing, is showing them a little respect."

Lionel's hands were always steady. Only once did I see them shake—just for a second—at Hamp's graveside, when

I told him I wished my husband had lived long enough to finish everything he'd started.

He hadn't changed much—lean and sharp-eyed, though the lines at the corners of his mouth dug in deeper now. He was checking a file when he looked up and saw me. His face broke into a smile.

"Well, if it isn't Mrs. Hampton Price." He set the papers down, came toward me, arms wide. "Come here, girl." He pulled me into a quick, rough hug.

"Got a minute?" I asked.

He glanced at the busy waiting room.

I felt guilty about taking up his time. But still. I'd be quick and I needed an answer. "It won't take long."

He hesitated, then nodded. Turned to the woman behind the desk. "I'll be right back."

We slipped down the hallway past the tired stares and restless feet. His office was a closet of a room stuffed with secondhand furniture and yellowing medical books. A battered desk fan pushed hot air around like it was doing somebody a favor.

He gestured toward a chair next to his desk and we both sat. He gave me an affectionate once-over. "It's good to see you, Lanie. Heard you're doing well."

"Well enough. And you? And the clinic?"

He shrugged. "Me, I'm fine. The clinic?" He raised an eyebrow and a wry smile worked his lips. "It has definitely seen better days."

There was a moment of awkward silence. His eyes lingered on me. I'd always sensed he had feelings for me. He was a lovely, handsome man. But those were feelings I couldn't return. Maybe that had also had a hand in why I'd stayed away.

He inclined his head. "But you're not here to see about me—or the clinic, are you?"

There it was—the little edge, small but sharp, like a blade he couldn't keep buried. I remembered now. It had always found its way out, sooner or later.

"I'm sorry, Lionel. Sorry I didn't keep in touch. I—"

He cut the air between us with a hand. "Doesn't matter."

His mouth said one thing. His tone said another. "What can I do for you?"

I drew a breath. "It's about Hamp."

"Of course."

The blade flashed sharper. I let it pass.

"Did he know?"

A loose sheet of paper lifted and fell on the desk from the fan's lazy push. Somewhere out front, a baby started to cry.

Lionel sighed. "I figured you'd come and ask sooner or later." He thought a second, then nodded. "Yeah. He knew."

My fingers tightened around my clutch. "He didn't tell me."

"No, he didn't. He didn't tell me half of it either. Thought he could outrun it."

The fan squealed on its stand. Feet impatiently shuffled in the hallway.

"He thought he was protecting you." Lionel's voice grew quieter, like the words cost him. "He thought if he just kept moving, he could give you a few more good years."

Now, it was my turn to give a slow nod. My tone that took on the bite.

"Well, it didn't work out that way, did it?"

"No, m'am. It did not."

I stood. I'd learned everything I wanted to know.

He rose with me. Opened his mouth, like maybe he

meant to say more. But settled for: "You ever need anything. You know where to find me."

I nodded. That was all I could manage.

The waiting room was thicker now, the air loaded with sweat and perfume and cigarette smoke. I didn't look at anybody as I slipped out the door. The sun hit like a hammer. The city smelled of tar and roasting garbage. I walked into it without a plan, my shoes striking hard against the pavement, the heat sinking deeper with every step.

42

The building creaked with night sounds—the radiator's sigh, the soft rattle of wind against the windows. Sam's office door was cracked open. I could see the light on. He was still here.

I didn't knock.

He was standing by the window, one hand resting on the frame, looking out at nothing.

"I thought you'd gone home," I said.

"I thought you had."

We stood in silence for a moment. Then I stepped inside and shut the door behind me.

"I went to see Sadie Wilkins."

That got his attention. He turned from the window. "And?"

"She was in love with him. With Westbrook."

Sam didn't respond. Just waited.

"She said he finally figured something out. Something he shouldn't have."

"About the sabotage?"

I nodded. "She thinks it got him killed."

"And you?"

"I think she's right."

He came back to his desk, but didn't sit. "You look like hell."

"Thanks."

"You okay?"

I considered lying. Then shook my head. "No. Not really."

Sam watched me for a long moment. Then he pulled a chair out and gestured for me to sit. I did. The silence between us settled like dust—soft, but everywhere.

"I keep going back over it," I said. "All of it. What Sadie said. What Westbrook must've known. He cared about that picture, Sam. About getting it right. And now he's dead and the story's trying to write itself without me."

"What do you mean?"

"I mean the official version is already forming. That he was unstable. Obsessed. Maybe guilty. That the pressure broke him. That's what management wants. That's what Seth probably wants. And the police? They're happy to call it suicide and be done."

"But you're not."

"No." I met his gaze. "Because I think he was murdered. And if I don't push, no one will."

Sam leaned back against his desk, crossed his arms. "You're not sleeping."

"No."

"You're not eating."

"Coffee counts."

"That's not funny."

"I wasn't joking."

Another silence.

Then, quietly: "You're scared."

"Wouldn't you be?"

He looked away. "I am."

That stopped me.

"I'm scared for you, Lanie. You're getting close. And the closer you get, the more dangerous this becomes."

I didn't answer right away.

"I used to think," he said, "that the worst thing would be if they silenced your story. But now? Now I think the worst thing would be if they silenced you."

The words hung there. No rescue in them. Just truth.

"I don't want to lose you," he said.

My throat tightened. I looked down at my hands. They didn't feel like mine anymore.

"I need to see this through," I said.

"I know."

He moved toward me. Not all the way. Just close enough.

"If you need help," he said, "ask for it. Don't pull the usual vanishing act. I don't want to find out something happened to you in tomorrow's paper."

"I'll be careful."

He didn't believe it. Neither did I.

But he nodded anyway.

I stood. We didn't touch. Didn't say anything more.

I left before the silence swallowed us both.

43

The bedroom I'd once shared with Hamp was dark except for a single candle flickering on the bedside table. I sat in my reading chair by the window with his photograph in my lap. Behind the cool glass of its silver frame, his face stared back at me.

I traced his jaw with my fingertip. Remembered how in those last months he'd pause at the top of our stairs, one hand pressed to his chest before continuing down. At the time, it seemed nothing—just a moment's rest after a long day at the hospital. Now each remembered gesture was a witness against me.

I'd given away all his clothes after the funeral. Everything except his favorite sweater. I rose, the photo clutched my hand and went to my closet. The box was where I'd left it, pushed far back on the top shelf. The wool was soft against my hands as I lifted it out.

"When are you going to get rid of that old thing?"

A smile. A chuckle. A "one-word answer: Never." Then a pause. "And I'll bet you a dollar that one day, you'll come to love it as much as I do."

I hadn't taken him up on that bet. But he was right. I had come to love it. In fact, I couldn't part with it.

I buried my nose in it and inhaled deeply. *Acqua di Parma*. Citrus and lavender, amber and musk. Hamp had bought a supply during our first trip to Italy. The scent unlocked a door in my mind.

"Sometimes things aren't as certain as we think," he'd said one evening.

I'd been too busy selecting the perfect shade of cream for the nursery walls, imagining the cradle we would place beneath the window.

"You're always worrying about nothing," I'd told him and returned to my color choices.

I paced the floor, sweater clutched against my chest. Every evening we'd spent in comfortable silence—him with medical journals spread across the parlor sofa, me at my desk nearby. Not knowing how precious those moments were.

"Life can be unpredictable, Lanie." His voice echoed in the empty room.

I'd always murmured agreement without looking up from my typewriter. We had all the time in the world.

Seth's words from earlier hit me. *"He tried to talk to me. More than once. But I was always so caught up in my dream that I wouldn't listen."*

The truth of it twisted like a knife. Hamp had tried to warn me. Again and again, he'd tried to get through.

"Sometimes hearts don't last forever," he'd said one night, hand resting over his chest.

"Don't be morbid," I'd said and kissed him, tasting coffee on his breath, never imagining it was his way of saying goodbye.

I had been too invested in our dreams, too determined to paint a rosy fantasy to see the stark reality.

"Lanie, promise me you'll take care of yourself." His eyes had searched mine for understanding I'd never given.

"Always," I'd assured him, thinking it just another of his endearing quirks.

My vision blurred and a sob tore from my throat. The photograph slipped from my fingers. and struck the hardwood floor. Its glass splintered with a soft crack.

I bent to pick it up but sagged to the floor. Through the broken glass, Hamp's smile seemed different now—not the confident grin of a young doctor with his whole life ahead, but something tender and sad. He'd known even then.

From somewhere down the street, Bessie Smith's voice floated through my open window. I couldn't make out the words, just the lament in her voice.

The candle sputtered and went out, leaving me in darkness.

"Maybe Sam is right not to trust me with his secrets," I whispered to the empty room. "I didn't even see the ones under my own roof."

44

"Lanie? This is Grace. Seth's throwing a party on set tonight. Nine sharp. To boost morale."

"A party? In the middle of all this chaos?"

"Seth's always been one for grand gestures," she said. A pause. "The jazz club set. Everyone will be there."

"Everyone, huh?" I drummed my fingers on my desk at the newsroom. Parties meant people. People meant gossip. And gossip meant secrets to be discovered. "Count me in. I'll be there. With bells on."

The ebony skies threatened rain as I entered the bustling party on the movie set warehouse that night. The air was thick with cigarette smoke, hooch and dust. Someone had put Ma Rainey on the phonograph and the sound of her blues filtered through the makeshift jazz club set, mixing with the clink of glasses and murmured conversations.

I swirled the ice in my gin rickey, weaving my way through the sea of faces,. The clink of glasses and murmur of voices filled the air, punctuated by occasional bursts of laughter.

Grace materialized from the smoke, a vision in gold silk and made the rest of the room look like a rehearsal.

"So glad you could make it." Her ruby lips curled into a smile, but her dark eyes remained guarded. "I've been thinking about our conversation. Have you had a chance to speak with Clay yet?"

"No, I was planning on speaking to him tonight—maybe set up an appointment tomorrow, when we can speak privately."

"That's good. Seth won't admit it, but I think he's glad to have someone from the outside, someone he trusts, who isn't a cop, who'll be discreet, you know..." She wound down. "I'm making a mess of this, but you know what I mean."

"I'll do my best. But I do intend to get a story out of it."

She sighed and nodded. "I know. But we also know, Seth and I, that you'll wait till it's safe to write it."

"That I'll do. I know how important this project is, not just to you and Seth, but to all of us. Bringing our stories to the screen is long overdue."

"I just wish everyone felt that way." She pursed her lips. "Seth's so well-meaning, but he has a habit of rubbing some people the wrong way. He's made his share of enemies. It's not just white Hollywood. In some cases, it's our own people. Folks who envy him, or want to use him—artistically and politically—to push their own views."

As she spoke, my gaze drifted across the room, the sounds of laughter and clinking glasses fading into the background. That's when I noticed him.

A pale-skinned man in a pinstriped suit, his slicked-back hair dark and gleaming under the lights. He was leaning on the bar, sipping a drink like he owned the place, measuring everything he saw against whatever price he had in mind.

"That guy over there," I nodded in his direction. "Do you know him?"

She followed my gaze, her brow furrowing. "Oh, good grief. What's he doing here?"

"Trouble?"

"He could be—if we let him. His name's Joe Dougherty. And he's a pickpocket."

"A what?"

"A pickpocket. A culture thief. One of those guys who go around, trying to buy up our work, then sell it as their own. He's after our movie script. I'm surprised he had the guts to show up here. Seth's already kicked him off the set at least twice. Seth's not violent, but I swear, the last time I thought he was going to punch the guy, just lay him out."

Everyone knew that colored filmmakers had a hard time attracting interest and backing in Hollywood. The studios often sidelined our talent and ignored our stories. There was a market for both, but Hollywood didn't think we were worth the bother. And also, there was the fear of offending people—the broader audience.

That didn't mean, however, that Hollywood wasn't interested in our ideas. It just wasn't interested in paying for them or giving us credit. Everybody'd heard of colored artists who'd seen their work taken by white producers. Of our songs, books and film scripts being adapted or outright stolen and then marketed to financial success—riches that bypassed us.

I started to press for more details when a familiar voice cut through the party chatter like a thunderclap.

"Dougherty!" Seth's voice cut through the party chatter like a thunderclap. "I told you to stay away from here!"

The room fell silent. The cacophony of voices, the clinking of glasses, even the distant rumble of traffic outside —all of it ceased in an instant. Every head turned towards the source of the outburst.

Seth stood in the doorway, his lean frame radiating fury. His fists were clenched at his sides, jaw set in a hard line. A dry cough rattled in his chest—short, sharp—but he didn't break stride.

Seth stormed across the room, his footsteps loud in the sudden hush. The crowd parted before him like the Red Sea, revealing Dougherty standing near the makeshift bar. His smug smile only seemed to fuel Seth's rage.

"You have no business here. Get out, now." Seth's voice was low, dangerous.

Dougherty raised his hands, palms out. "All right, all right. No need to make a scene. I was just leaving."

Seth's eyes blazed, reflecting the harsh glare of the overhead lights. "This project is too important to be tainted by the likes of you."

I glanced around, taking in the expressions of the others who were watching. I saw heads nodding, sometimes only slightly but still definitively. People were agreeing with Seth. Clay stood near the exit, leaning against the wall, watching with one eyebrow raised and shaking his head, as if he couldn't believe Dougherty's gall.

Dougherty shrugged, his nonchalance a deliberate provocation. "Can't blame a man for trying to make an honest living."

"Honest?" The word dripped acid. "There's nothing honest about stealing our stories, our culture, our very souls."

"Dougherty turned to leave, then paused and cut his eyes over to Clay. The look was quick but it said plenty.

Grace squeezed Seth's shoulder as conversation slowly resumed. I set down my glass and followed Clay's retreating form into the hallway. Sometimes the best stories hide in the shadows between what's said and what's left unspoken.

Thunder growled outside, real this time. I pressed against the cool concrete wall, inching forward as Clay's footsteps echoed ahead. The exit door groaned open, letting in the smell of rain-soaked asphalt. The coming storm matched the tension in my gut.

'Dougherty, wait.'

I peered around the doorframe. Clay stood rigid under the yellow streetlight, his shadow stretching long and dark across wet pavement. Dougherty's silhouette loomed closer, that knowing smirk still playing on his face. Their voices dropped low, but their bodies told the story - Clay's defensive stance softening into resignation, Dougherty's predatory lean.

The exchange itself was quick. A manila envelope passing from hand to hand, something else slipped into pockets. But it was Clay's posture that told the real tale - the way his shoulders curved inward like a man who'd just signed away his birthright.

Dougherty tucked the envelope inside his pinstriped jacket, patted it once like he was sealing a bargain. He walked away whistling while Clay stood alone in the falling rain, one hand still in his pocket where whatever Dougherty had given him burned like broken promises.

The first real drops of rain began to fall as Clay turned back toward the door. I slipped away before he could spot me, my mind churning with questions I wasn't sure I wanted answered.

45

I shut the door and stood there a beat, hand still on the knob. I didn't know what I was hoping to find. Only that Sadie had put something in my head that wouldn't shake loose. Westbrook found something at that hotel. Something small enough to fit in his hand. Small enough to hide.

The air still carried him. Tobacco. Coffee. A trace of something older—cologne maybe. The bulb overhead buzzed. Its sway cast jagged shadows across the shelves—cameras, lenses, spools of film. Reels lined up like forgotten promises.

I didn't move. Just listened. The silence wasn't empty. It held shape, as if someone had just left the room but left the door open behind them. Like the place was waiting. And it knew I'd come.

It looked mostly the way I remembered it—but only mostly.

I'd only been in here once, but the order had stood out. Westbrook kept things precise. Cameras lined up. Lenses capped. Reels stacked tight along the edge of the shelf.

Now the symmetry had slipped.

The cameras and lenses and film were slightly askew. The reels nudged out of place. His lighting diagrams were scattered in with script drafts, turned this way and that. The couch cushions had been lifted and dropped back without care. The lens case beneath the window gaped open, two trays pulled out and left at angles—as if someone had started to reach, then thought better of it.

Quiet hands. Careful. But not careful enough.

I stood still and let the silence settle.

Whoever had searched this place hadn't wrecked it. No drawers yanked out. No papers scattered across the floor. But something had been broken all the same.

Westbrook worked in straight lines. Lighting ratios. Shot lists. Framing down to the inch. He made order out of chaos.

Now that order had been undone. Quietly. Deliberately.

I hadn't known him well. We'd spoken twice. But even when I thought he might be behind the sabotage, I liked him. And once I heard what Sadie had to say—about the film, about what they'd shared—I saw him for what he was.

A man trying to make something good before the lights went out.

This room was the last place his hands had moved.

And now even that had been touched.

Not ruined.

Quietly dismantled.

The desk hadn't been ransacked, but it had been touched. I flipped through the paperwork on his desk. Nothing unusual there. No hidden items. Big or small.

The top drawer sat open half an inch. I pulled it wider. Batteries. Pencils. Film spools. A pair of worn work gloves. No tools.

I checked each drawer, one by one. Most were surprisingly empty. Something about that bothered me, but I couldn't put my finger on it. I ran my fingers along the seams, pressed for false bottoms. Bent low and felt beneath. Nothing taped there. Just dust and old wood.

I moved on to the shelves, checked the cameras and their accessories. If Westie had hidden anything there, it was gone.

I turned to the tall cabinet by the shelves. Its latch was bent—barely—but enough to catch my eye. I tested the top door. It opened stiffly.

Did Westbrook leave it unlocked? Or did someone force it?

My toe touched something on the floor: a pair of pliers. *Well, that answers that question.* I picked it up, checked the cabinet lock. It was slightly bent and scored.

I opened the top door: Empty camera boxes. Two light meters, both set at different readings—like someone had tested them and left them behind. A velvet-lined pouch lay open, its drawstring tangled. A few labeled containers of developing fluid, one missing its cap. Still tidy, but not untouched.

I crouched and opened the lower door.

Lighting gels spilled forward in a loose heap. Some were bent at the edges, like they'd been jammed back in a rush. A narrow zippered kit bag had been upturned and dumped on the cabinet floor. Its contents—lens cloths and brushes, a loupe, a screwdriver, measuring tape and electrical tape— lay jumbled and exposed. A bulb had rolled loose and come to rest against the back wall.

I reached past the mess and ran my hand along the cabinet wall. Smooth. No false panel. No hidden box.

I stood. Straightened my skirt. Turned slowly.

Everything on the outer surfaces looked mostly as I'd first seen it. But now I could feel it.

Whoever had searched this room had done it in stages.

Quiet. Controlled. Until something shifted. Until time got short. Or nerves frayed.

They hadn't turned the place inside out. But they'd stopped being careful.

I went to the sofa. I knew that was what the searcher had done. Lifted one cushion. Ran a hand along the frame. Lifted the second, flipped it quickly, nails scratching along the lining.

Found nothing. Slapped the cushions back into place. One landing crooked; the other partially unzipped. Past caring. Leaving it that way.

Gaze traveling over the room. Knowing he'd left signs. Not caring anymore. Because he was running out of places to look.

Or maybe he'd already missed it.

I stood. Stepped back. That's when I noticed the waste-basket. I mentally kicked myself for not seeing it before, but it was in a blind spot, sitting in shadow on one side of the desk.

Film wrappers. A broken pencil. A crumpled newspaper report about the Klan's march on Washington. Thousands in white robes, parading past the Capitol like they had a right to be there.

And beneath that— several pages, ripped apart and folded over, then ripped again. But the fragments were still big enough to fit back together. Westbrook's copy of his financing agreement with Seth. The signature had been torn straight through.

Whoever had been here hadn't just searched. They'd wanted this gone.

Was it Seth? He was short on funding now. Could he have found this document, tried to destroy it? Erase any record that he owed Westie money—money he either couldn't pay back or profit he didn't want to share?

Why not destroy evidence of that debt? After all, Westie had no heirs. This was probably the only copy of the document. No one would look for it.

I straightened up, still holding the pages and as I did I saw the photograph. Him and Seth, years ago. Seth just a boy, grinning wide, arm slung around his instructor's shoulders. I'd been so intent on the desk itself, I'd barely noticed the image above it.

But now I did. Call it pity. Call it sorrow. Call it something else. But I felt drawn to that photo, as if an unseen hand were pulling me in.

At first I couldn't understand why. The subject was heartbreaking, of course. Westbrook and Seth were smiling like they had the world in front of them. Seeing them, you'd never guess that their friendship would end in death for one and possible ruin for the other.

But it wasn't just the image that drew me.

I stepped closer and as I did, I heard it—a soft crunch under my heel.

I looked down. A sliver of glass. And another. Not far from the baseboard, tucked near the leg of the desk.

I looked back at the frame.

The glass was gone. But small jagged edges stuck out from the frame. The photo still standing, undisturbed, as if nothing had happened.

But something had.

Had Seth done this? Bashed the photo against Westie's desk, then regretted it, hid the broken pieces of glass and set the image where it belonged again.

That's how it looked. That's what it would look like to someone investigating.

I let my gaze drift, taking in the room again.

Then I saw it—the lamp on the edge of the desk. Ornate thing. Satin shade. Crystal tassels.

Westbrook had been hunched over it that first day we spoke. His broad shoulders pulled in, fingers working one of the crystals with a pair of pliers. Hands too big for that kind of task, but precise. I'd thought it looked too delicate for him. Maybe a film prop. But what would a senior cameraman be doing with a film prop?

I stepped closer and brushed my fingers across the fringe. The tassels swayed, catching light in a slow shimmer. I ran my hand along the row of crystals, letting them tick softly against my skin. A steady rhythm, almost soothing.

Then I leaned in. Studied the cut of each piece.

And there it was.

Not hidden. Not tucked away. Just nestled among the others. A shade off. A fraction smaller. But hung the same way. Same bounce. Same polish.

It didn't belong.

I reached for it. Stopped.

Looked around—desk, drawers, shelves. There were those pliers on the floor. I thought about using them but knowing me I'd do more damage than good with them. Instead, I took a hairpin from my hair and went to work.

The wire was twisted tight. Westie had made sure it was secure. I eased the pin into the loop and worked slowly, careful not to snap the metal or leave a mark.

It took time.

Finally, the tension gave.

I caught the piece before it fell. Turned it over in my hand. Small. Elegant. Inconspicuous. Meaningless—unless you knew.

I closed my fingers around it. Westbrook had found this. He'd known what it meant.

And it had cost him.

I didn't hear anything, but I felt it. The air had shifted. Lighter. Or maybe just less burdened.

As if someone had been waiting for me to find this— small in size, heavy with meaning.

I slipped it into my pocket.

Near the desk, the wastebasket sat where I'd left it. I reached in, lifted the torn pages and folded them flat. They weren't mine. But they mattered.

The photograph still stood on the shelf. No glass. One hard knock away from being lost. I moved it to the desk, out of harm's way.

Then I looked at the lamp. At the chair. At what was left of him.

In my head, I heard him. That dry rasp, steady and low. *You know what to do with it, don't you?*

And I answered. *I do—and I will.*

46

The humid air clung to my skin as I approached Seth on the bustling movie set. Sweat beaded on my forehead and I could taste the salt on my lips. The acrid smell of cigarette smoke mingled with the musty scent of old wood from the makeshift jazz club set.

"Seth, I've been thinking about your script. I'd love to take a closer look, if you're willing. You have my word I won't leak anything."

Seth's frowned, considering. "I don't know, Lanie. It's risky."

"C'mon. Trust me. I'm here to help, remember?"

A moment passed before his posture relaxed. "All right. But be careful with it.."

We made our way through the chaos of the set, dodging crew members and piles of equipment to reach his office. In a quiet corner, Seth pulled a thick stack of papers from his bag.

"Here," he said, handing me the script. "But be careful with it."

As I flipped through the pages, the paper rough against

my fingers, certain things jumped out at me. The typefaces shifted between scenes. Some were crisp and professional; others were slightly askew with occasional typos.

I turned back to Seth, the script's pages rustling softly under my fingers. "These typefaces ... they're different throughout. Why is that?"

Seth nodded. "Yes. Clay and I, we wrote it together. Different typewriters, you see." He leaned in, pointing at a particular page.

As he bent closer, I caught the faint rasp in his breathing —barely noticeable over the racket of the set, but there.

"These scenes here? All mine. You can tell by the crooked 'e' and ... well, the spelling." He gave a rueful smile and shrugged. "I never could spell."

I traced my finger along the lines, feeling the indentations left by the keys. "Interesting. I couldn't imagine sharing a column, that kind of collaboration."

"It's not easy, but we make it work. I have to give credit where credit is due, though. Clay is the details, man. I have the 'grand vision,'"—he made air quotes—"but he's the one who makes them work. I don't know where I'd be without him."

As a child, I'd yearned for a sibling. Seth's words reminded me of that never-fulfilled desire. Listening to him, I felt a whiff of the old sadness. I drew a deep breath and refocused on the moment. I needed samples of both typefaces, but how to obtain them without arousing suspicion?

Before I could come up with a plan, the office door opened and Grace Carter stuck her head in. "Seth, a word, please?"

Seth's brow furrowed. He glanced at me apologetically. "Excuse me, Lanie. I'll be right back."

The moment he closed the door behind him, I hurried

to his desk and grabbed a sheet of typing paper. Working fast, I rolled the page into his typewriter and typed a line of the alphabet, then ripped the sheet out, scurried over to Clay's desk and did the same with his typewriter. I now had examples of the typeface from both typewriters and knew which typeface came from which.

I pounded the keys, typing fast. The keys clunked loudly; it would be hard to explain what I was doing if someone heard the noise and walked in the door.

I straightened up, pulse pounding, slipped the sheet of paper into my purse and stepped away from Clay's desk. Just as I did, he opened the door and walked in. He came to a halt at the sight of me.

"Miss Lanie. What're you doing in here? Waiting for my brother?" His eyes narrowed. "And is that our script you have in your hand?"

I explained how Seth had kindly shared it with me. Clay was about to ask another question when Seth returned. His arrival provided a welcome distraction.

"Oh, Clay, glad you're here." Seth shut the door. "I wanted to talk to you about something. About Joe Dougherty being there last night ... the gall of that man. Any idea how he could've found out about the party?"

Clay shrugged. "Probably somebody on the crew told him. They say he's got spies everywhere."

"Yeah, but I'd hate to think he's gotten to one of us."

I spoke up. "Dougherty's offer, why'd you turn it down, Seth?" I could guess the answer to my question, but I wanted to hear it from Seth.

Clay's eyes flashed. "We don't want anything to do with him or his offers."

"Well, I hope he got the message. Finally," Seth sighed.

A wry smile played on Clay's lips. "I think so. I went after him and told him flat-out that if he shows up again, we'll have his legs broken."

Seth's eyebrows shot up. "You didn't."

"I sure did," Clay laughed. "I was just joking. But I knew he'd believe that a colored man would do something like that, use violence."

Both brothers laughed at that. It was a good moment, a break in the tension that otherwise ruled the set.

The late afternoon sun slanted through the office windows, spilling across the desks like a last chance.

I spoke to Seth. "Those threatening notes you mentioned, I'd like to take a look at them."

Seth frowned. "Why?"

"I'd just like to check them. I promise to return them."

"You're not going to show them to the police, are you, or publish them in the paper?"

"No, of course not."

His eyes darted to Clay, then back to me. I could almost see the gears turning in his mind.

"I won't show them to anyone. I promise."

He exhaled slowly, then nodded. "All right. Two. That's all."

He retrieved them from his desk and handed them over. I carefully folded them and tucked them away, alongside the sheet of paper I'd typed earlier. The truth was waiting there, hidden in the typefaces and threatening scrawls.

The bustle of the Bronx streets enveloped me as I left the set. Car horns blared and the acrid smell of exhaust mixed with the enticing aroma of a nearby deli. But I barely noticed, my thoughts consumed by the evidence burning a hole in my purse.

Back in my office, I spread everything out on my desk: the script pages, the threatening notes. I studied them, comparing fonts, searching for spelling patterns. The ticking of my desk clock faded into the background as I lost myself in the analysis.

Minutes passed. The pieces started falling into place. The truth was there, staring me in the face, but it was one I wasn't sure I wanted to see. I thought of Hamp, of the secret he'd kept from me. And I could hear Seth, describing the people he worked with as close as family. How well did we ever really know the people we trusted?

I leaned back in my chair. I knew what I had to do next. And I knew it wouldn't be easy.

47

F unny thing about people—how they can look right past what's in front of them. Not out of malice, no. More like... habit. They get caught up in their own rhythm, their own plans, believing that the people beside them will keep step. They forget that sometimes, even the closest ones can start to drift away.

It's not always the big betrayals that do the damage. No, it's the small things. The words left unsaid. The looks that linger a second too long, or don't linger long enough. Those moments when you assume that everything is fine, because it's easier than facing the alternative—that maybe, just maybe, it's not.

Some people think they've got all the time in the world to mend those cracks. They think they can make things right, that they'll get a chance to fix what's gone wrong. But time has a way of slipping through your fingers. And when you finally see the truth staring back at you, it's too late to change it. Too late to take back the things you never said. The things you never saw.

Maybe it's a best friend, who never tells you how the

silence eats away at her until she can't hold it in any longer. Or the person who waits for you, year after year, hoping you'll find a way to let him in. Either way, the story's the same: a dream, a promise and the pieces that fall apart when nobody's paying attention.

You can build something strong—something that feels like it'll last forever—but even the strongest things have their breaking point. And when they break, you're left wondering if you could've seen it coming, if there was a moment when you could've reached out a hand, could've pulled them back before they slipped away.

But the truth is, we're all blind in our own way. To what we're losing. To what's slipping through the cracks. To the people who needed us most, standing right beside us, waiting to be seen.

And when you finally see it—when you realize what's been lost—it hits you like a punch you never saw coming. You think about what could have been, if only you'd paid a little more attention. If only you'd listened. But all you can do is stand there, staring at the pieces, wondering if it's too late to pick them up.

48

The murky shadows of the empty movie set, made to replicate a jazz club, cast long shadows across Clay's face as he settled into the rickety folding chair. He and I sat together, just the two of us on the stage, facing one another, like old friends having an intimate conversation. The musty scent of old fabric and sawdust mingled with the acrid tang of cigarette smoke that clung to his clothes.

"Thank you for meeting me," I said. "I know how busy you are."

He waved a dismissive hand. "Of course, I would. This movie is as important to me as it is to my brother."

"I appreciate that. I just wanted to let you know that I've finally figured it out—not all of it, perhaps, but most of it."

Clay's eyes lit up. "So you're finally satisfied that Westwood was behind the sabotage? And that when he was found out, he ducked out?"

"Not so fast. Let me walk you through what I found."

I described the pipe and what it told me. Clay's brow furrowed in thought and he nodded, following my logic. But when I told him how Seth approached me on the catwalk, so aggressive that he frightened me, Clay drew back and frowned. A faint smile of disbelief bowed his lips, as if to say, *Come on. You must be joking.*

"Seth told me you thought you'd found something. But now you're telling me you actually suspect him? Is that what this is all about? Is that why you wanted me to meet you here alone? Cause if it is, if that's it—that you suspect Seth —then you're out of your mind and I won't sit here and listen you dirty his name."

He stood to leave and I reached out a hand to calm him.

"No. Not him," I said. "He's not the one who did this, who killed Westwood—and Westwood wasn't the one behind the sabotage."

Clay inclined his head, his eyes wary. After a moment, he sat back down, but he was tense, back ramrod straight. "All right," he said. "Let's have it."

"I also spoke with Grace."

His head snapped up. "Grace? You couldn't possibly think she'd have anything to do with this. That's not her style."

I raised a calming hand. "Actually, she did have a potential motive—a good one. But it turns out she has an even stronger reason to protect the film."

"And what's that?"

"The chance to gain her own theater." I shared what Grace had told me. "She certainly seems to believe that Seth will keep his word. And she definitely wouldn't try to destroy his means to keep it."

He let out a low whistle. "Well, I'll be damned."

"You didn't know? I assumed Seth would've told you."

He shook his head. "No, he didn't. But, it makes sense, him giving her that money. It would certainly change things for her."

I watched him process this information, saw how he understood the import.

A new wariness entered his dark eyes. "So, if you don't think it was Westie and it's not Seth or Grace ... then who do you suspect? One of the actors? Someone else on the crew?"

I met his gaze, feeling oddly calm, even dispassionate. "That, I'm afraid, is exactly what this meeting is all about."

He leaned back, crossing his arms. A flicker of fear crossed his face, but it vanished as quickly as it appeared. His dark eyes narrowed, full of cunning.

The answer was obvious. I said nothing.

That slow smile of disbelief touched his lips again. "C'mon. You can't believe—you can't be saying you think it's me?" He touched his chest in innocent surprise.

"You've been doubling as Westbrook's camera assistant, correct?"

"Yes, I—" His eyes widened. "Wait a minute. What are you getting at?"

"I'm not 'getting at' anything. Merely presenting facts. And the facts are these: that you had the access and the skills to commit the sabotage."

He shot to his feet, his chair scraping against the concrete floor. "You're accusing me?! That's rich! Why, I would never—"

"Of course, you would," I interrupted, holding up a hand. "You would—and you did. There is evidence and it all points to you." My tone changed. "Now, sit down."

He opened his mouth to speak, but nothing came out. Instead, he dropped down in his chair like a stone held by gravity. He had to listen. He didn't want to, but he had to. Pride and panic kept him nailed in place.

I explained about the typefaces, watching his face contort with disbelief and anger. "The typeface used in the notes matches the one used in the pages that came from your typewriter."

"This is absurd." He jumped up and began pacing back and forth. "I've dedicated my life to this film, to my brother's vision. How can you sit there and say I'd sabotage it?!"

He should've been an actor. Then again, aren't all writers actors at heart? At least, in their minds, when they're putting together characters, coming up with plots? Imagining crimes they have their characters commit? As for Clay, he was more than an armchair actor. He was, in many ways, the real thing. After all, he had to have been, to have worn the mask and carried out the charade he'd put up for all these years. To have hid how he truly felt ...

His protests echoed off the bare walls. I let him rail on for a few minutes. Then I took a deep breath, the musty scent of the old set filling my lungs and continued.

"The typeface used in the notes ties them to your type-writer. But it's their content that ties them to you."

"You're out of your mind."

"I'm creative, yes, but not like you. The notes, you see, were flawless. Not a single typo or misspelling anywhere. But the pages from Seth's typewriter? They're a different story: littered with errors and corrections."

Clay came to a halt. His dark eyes were wide with resentment and something else—fear, perhaps? "So what?" His voice was barely above a whisper.

"So ... Seth's pages are the product of a busy mind, a visionary so caught up in the forest that he doesn't see the trees. Your pages reflect the opposite. They're the product of a very focused mind, a mind like yours, one so intent on the details, the trees, that it loses sight of the big picture, the forest."

A bead of sweat rolled down his temple. He opened his

mouth to speak, then closed it again. He grimaced, searching for something to say, then finally squeezed out four words. "I didn't do it."

He had so much to lose. He'd gambled it all, risked it all. What else was he going to say?

"There's more, Clay." I watched him closely. "I saw you with Joe Dougherty."

His head snapped up, eyes narrowing. "Dougherty? What's he got to do with this?"

"Everything," I said. "I spoke to him. He was reluctant at first—of course, he would be about talking to a reporter—but when I told him what was what, that the effort to ruin this movie production was risking lives, he sounded shocked."

Clay rubbed his face. "You're bluffing—or he's lying. We didn't—"

"He confirmed your deal, but said he didn't know anything about how you were going about it—and now that he did know, he wanted nothing to do with you or your 'damn' script. His words, not mine. Apparently, he's greedy —but not that greedy, not enough to kill or risk killing another human being."

Clay looked as if he were running out of air. He tugged at his shirt collar. Again, he managed to squeeze out just four words.

"I don't believe you."

"You don't have to. Call him. Or try to. I doubt he'll take your calls anymore."

Clay's remaining composure cracked. He stumbled back a couple of steps and caught himself on the edge of a prop table. The clatter of falling objects punctuated the heavy silence. His shoulders slumped. In that moment, I saw not the saboteur, but a man trapped by his own choices, choices as suffocating as the humid air around us.

"You don't understand," he whispered. "Dear God, why does no one else understand? See what I see? You accuse me of not seeing the forest for the trees. Lady, it's the other way around. It's Seth's who's lost sight of the big picture, not me. He's so damned naive. This dream of his? It's a fool's errand. And my brother—I love him—but he's a fool for chasing after it."

"His dream. Not yours. So you decided to destroy it?"

His laugh was bitter. "You still don't understand, do you? I wasn't trying to destroy his dream? I was trying to *save* it— save *us*. So we could survive and fight another day."

"And the only way to do that was through a deal with the devil?"

"Damn straight it was."

For a moment there, I wondered if he actually believed in what he was saying, wondered who he was trying to convince—me or himself—to justify what he must've known deep down was wrong.

"One last question," I said. I'd never believed that Wilkie could've provided all that information Selena had—or that she had the imagination to fabricate *all* of the quotes she mentioned. "The stories—the newspaper stories. You were the other unnamed source, weren't you?"

He said nothing, but his lips curved into a small grim smile.

Thunder rumbled in the distance, a fitting backdrop to the tension crackling between us. His face lit with a sudden thought. His eyes slid back to me. He came back, sat down and regarded me with contempt. "You know you've got nothing, right? Those notes, the typewriter ...?" He dismissed them with a wave of his hand. "If you can get anybody to listen—and that's a big if, then I can explain it all away." He shrugged. "You're a pretty smart lady. I've got to give you that. But you got outdone on this one." He leaned closer, grinning in my face. "You can't prove a thing."

"I don't have to. You've already done it for me."

He frowned, confusion marking his handsome face. "What're you talking about?"

I paused, considering him, considering what he'd gone through—and was about to go through. I almost felt sorry for him.

Almost.

I uttered the one word that would change everything: "Lights!"

The set suddenly blazed with illumination. Clay blinked, momentarily blinded. Then his eyes adjusted. He looked around, saw what he saw—and his mouth sagged open.

49

The spotlight cut through the darkness, freezing Clay where he stood. His eyes widened in disbelief, shoulders pulling back as though bracing against a blow. For a fleeting moment, his gaze darted to the exit, the barest hint of panic flashing across his face before he masked it with defiance.

He whirled on me. "You set me up."

I almost shrugged, but that would've been rude. Instead, I simply spoke the truth, "No. You did this to yourself."

"Clay," Seth stepped forward, his footsteps echoing in the cavernous space. "I had to hear it from you. To believe it. To understand why."

Clay's hands trembled, his fingers curling into fists at his sides, his chest rising and falling rapidly with each shallow breath. "I did this for us. You were risking everything on a dream."

The words, so accusatory, were a self-serving inversion of the idealism that had brought them all there. I wanted to feel some sympathy for Clay, because for him, those words were perhaps the truth, his version of it, anyway. But it was difficult to find understanding or pity for him. How could he not see the magnitude of what he'd done?

"And you were willing to destroy that dream," Seth said, "not just for me but for everyone involved. You put lives at risk."

A bead of sweat trickled down Clay's temple.

Grace emerged from the darkness. Her eyes flashed with disappointment and fury. "How could you? After all we sacrificed? We trusted you."

Clay shrunk back, his shoulders hunched as if to ward off a physical blow.

"I thought you believed in this project, in Seth's vision," Grace said.

Clay's face contorted, a desperate plea in his eyes. "I did," he choked out, "but ..."

The unfinished sentence dangled between us, as fragile as a cobweb. I found myself holding my breath, waiting for the explanation that could somehow justify his actions. But seconds passed and none came.

"But what?" Seth finally asked.

For a moment, I thought I saw a flicker of remorse in Clay's eyes. But then his jaw clenched, defiance overtaking guilt.

"You don't understand," he spat. "None of you do. Always in Seth's shadow, always the afterthought. Do you know what it's like to pour your heart and soul into something, only to have someone else be given all the credit?"

"So you thought selling out was the answer?" Grace asked.

Clay flinched as if she'd slapped him. "I didn't ... I wasn't ..."

His protests died on his lips. The reality of what he'd done settled over him and the spotlight seemed to grow brighter, harsher, exposing every line of anguish on his face.

"So, Clay," Seth said, "did you kill Westie?"

Clay's eyebrows shot up in panic. He held out a hand as if to ward off the accusation. "No! No, of course not."

"I'm going to ask you again," Seth said. "Did you ... do it?"

Clay licked his lips and held his head. "I did not. I ... didn't have a hand in that."

Seth frowned. "Look, you already admitted to—"

I spoke up. "He's telling the truth, Seth. Yes, he's a saboteur, but he didn't commit murder." I nodded to the person sitting at Seth's side. "I'm afraid she did that."

There was a shocked silence. Seth's jaw sagged. He glanced at Grace, who'd blanched. Seth took a sudden, shallow breath and coughed once, hard, into the crook of his arm.

"How dare you?!" Grace cried.

I turned back to Clay. "Are you going to let her get away it? Are you willing to go to jail while she walks free? Because you will go to jail, you know. The police will think that you killed Westbrook because he found out that you were the saboteur. No one will look twice at her. All they'll do is look at you."

Clay looked at Grace. Her nostrils flared and returned his look with slight shake of her head.

Seth caught the unspoken communication between them. "Clay?" he asked. "Grace?"

Still nothing.

Seth's face showed a dawning realization—that while he may have been shocked, Clay clearly wasn't.

Clay's gaze shifted between Grace and Seth, back and

forth, back and forth, as he tried to make up his mind. All eyes remained trained on him.

Finally, he licked his lips and spoke to his brother. "She did it. She tried to get me to do it, but I wouldn't. I said I couldn't go there. So she did it instead."

There was a moment of explosive silence. Then Grace jumped up, jabbing an accusatory finger at Clay. "Why you lying son-of-a-bitch! You got caught and now you're trying to blame me—me, of all people. I've done nothing but fight for this film. Why the hell would I do such a thing—kill Westie?"

"Because he was going to tell on us," Clay said. "He knew that we were having an affair—"

"You *what*?" Seth's voice was strangled.

"You heard me," Clay said. "We were ... involved. For more than a month now. Westbrook found out. Told Grace. Said he was going to warn you."

"You low-down dirty dog," Grace snapped. "You're a liar! You even lie for a living! No one's gonna believe you—no one!"

"Maybe not," Clay said, oddly calm. "But they'll believe the letters you sent me. The ones where you wrote about what we did together when Seth wasn't looking and how we'd spend his money when he's gone."

"I never said nothing like that!"

Clay's smile was slight but triumphant. He'd trapped her, provoked her into admitting the letters existed, even as she disputed their contents.

Grace gasped, clapping a hand over her mouth, but it was too late. The damage was done. She'd fallen into a trap, expertly set and expertly sprung. And we all knew it.

She lifted her chin, eyes flashing, moving between Seth

and me as if daring either of us to judge her. Her tone was
both proud and bitter.

"Fine. Let's put it all out there. I did what had to be done.
Clay refused. He was too damn weak to do what was necessary, so I did it myself." Her gaze flicked to me. "It was the
only way. That old man would've ruined everything."

I didn't respond, only raised an eyebrow and glanced at
Seth. This wasn't about me—it was Seth who she needed to
face, to convince. And it was to him she finally turned, her
tone softening, almost pleading.

"You do see that, don't you, hon? If he'd told you about
the affair, you would've turned on me, refused to give me the
money for my playhouse."

Seth's expression said it all. He looked hollowed out,
gutted, like he was staring at a stranger. "Who are you?" he
whispered. "Who the hell are you?"

Grace swallowed, faltering as her face paled. She opened
her mouth to speak, to explain, but something in Seth's eyes
stopped her cold.

"This project," he said. "You working on it with me. The
money. Was that what it was all about? The money?"

"No! No, of course not! You know me better than that,
Seth."

"Do I? Because right now, I'm thinking I don't know you
at all."

"Don't say that! I poured my heart and soul into this film.
I believed in it—in you. But I was always honest with you.
Always told you that I needed to have something of my
own."

Seth didn't respond. His eyes fixed on her as if searching
for someone who no longer existed.

She hesitated, casting a quick, almost involuntary look
at Clay. She shifted, her voice lowering, almost breaking.

"And I didn't know about the sabotage. I honestly thought it was Westbrook—that he was behind it. If I'd known Clay was responsible, I would've stopped him, I swear it. But I didn't know. Not until just now."

"Why?" Seth's gaze shifted between the two of them. "Why? You two, together? Why?"

Grace pressed her lips together. Several seconds of tense silence passed. It was Clay who finally spoke up.

"There is no 'why,'" Clay shrugged. "It simply 'was.' It was a thing that happened. That's all. It. Just. Happened."

"And how many times," Seth asked, "did it 'happen?'"

Grace swallowed.

Clay waved away the question. "C'mon man, you don't want to know—"

"The hell I don't!" Seth's hands balled into fists and the tendons in his neck strained. "How. Many. *Times?*"

Clay wouldn't answer. He still had enough decency to look ashamed and, under the pressure of Seth's angry stare, averted his gaze.

Seth looked to Grace. Their gazes held.

"Does it matter?" she finally said.

Seth looked as though she'd struck him. Something died inside him. I could see it in his eyes. "No," he said, "I guess it doesn't."

"I *am* sorry," she said. "About me and Clay and ... about Westbrook, too. I thought he was behind the sabotage."

But Seth wasn't buying it. "Don't try to lie now. You already admitted it. You did it because you couldn't risk him telling me the truth. You've told me the 'why.' Now, tell me the 'how.' How did you do it, Grace? What exactly did you do?"

She lowered her gaze for a moment, collecting herself, before she spoke again, more to herself than anyone else.

"After the argument, I contacted him, told him to meet me here. I'd already offered him money, but he'd turned it down. Said the only thing that would satisfy him was my telling you the truth. So, I told him that that's what I was going to do. Said I wanted to thank him for not saying anything to you. Even when you were yelling at him, telling him to leave, he said nothing."

She faltered, a note of genuine surprise in her voice. "Shocked me, really. But the very fact that he didn't say anything told me he *would* if I didn't give in to him. That he was serious and I had one last chance to settle this—settle it permanently. So I did. It was easy, actually." She paused and again expressed bewilderment. "You see, despite everything, he trusted me."

Westbrook. Tough and seasoned and cynical, yet soft-hearted enough to give this lying woman a chance, if not for her sake, then for Seth's—a trust she'd used against him. Another betrayal and a particularly horrible one at that. It had cost the gruff old cameraman his life.

Grace gave in to a little shiver and hugged herself, as if she'd felt a chill—or that something dark and irreversible had crossed her path. With a sudden resolve, she looked at Seth. Her next words came out a soft, broken whisper.

"I did it for the both of us, hon. He was going to tell you. I told him the news would kill you. But he didn't want to listen. He just kept saying that a man in your state had a right to know."

Seth closed his eyes. The pain on his face was raw, as if her words had stripped away the last of his faith in her, killed any last hope that she hadn't done this. His voice, when he spoke, was barely more than a whisper, but each word was edged with fury and grief.

"You killed someone, Grace. Actually killed someone.

And it wasn't just anyone. It was someone we knew. I can't ... I can't get past that. That old man... he and I, we had our differences—for sure—but he was like a father to me."

He lightly touched the area over his heart. "I wouldn't be who I am, done what I've managed to do, without him. I *loved* him—and you knew it. You *knew* that."

"I did it for you—"

"The hell you did!" Seth took a shuddering breath. "The thing is, killing him was not only wrong; it was *unnecessary*. I could've forgiven you, Grace. Forgiven both of you, for the affair. People make mistakes. But murder?" He shook his head. "You crossed the line and there's no coming back from that."

That verdict, quietly delivered in the cavernous silence of that dark warehouse, reverberated with the weight of a court judgment.

Seth closed his eyes and for a moment, his face twisted with a pain too deep to disguise. When he looked at his brother again, his voice was calm but edged with raw sorrow. "I can forgive you, Clay... but I can't trust you. Not anymore."

His voice held the finality of a prison sentence. This wasn't just about betrayal; it was about consequences.

"You have a choice," Seth said. "Surrender your rights to the script and go away. Forever. Go somewhere where you can start over, figure out what you really want."

Clay was stunned. "Seth, no—"

"It's that," Seth said, "or face prosecution for what you did, for the danger and the damage you caused."

Clay's face drained of color. He licked his lips, then took a weak step forward, his hands spread in supplication. "Please, don't ... Don't do this."

The desperation in his voice was palpable. This was the

ugly truth of ambition gone awry, of dreams corrupted by greed.

Seth held up a hand, silencing his brother. The gesture was gentle, but carried the gravity of a judge's gavel. "You have until tomorrow to decide."

Two people he loved dearly had plotted against him. One had already been dealt with. Now, it was time to handle the other.

A dark figure emerged from the shadows behind us, followed by two officers. As he stepped into light, his short, stocky figure became easily recognizable. He glanced at me with a reluctant glint of respect in his eye. He nodded, his grin smug.

"I have to say, I didn't believe you, Price. Nearly didn't come. You promised me a show. Didn't think you'd deliver, but I have to say, this was definitely worth the price of admission."

Arnold chuckled as if savoring the moment. It was a nasty little sound and I didn't like the sound of it. Heck, I wasn't even sure whether I liked him, but I was glad he was there.

His gaze took in each of the players in this little drama: Seth, Grace and finally Clay. His eyes dwelled on Clay the longest and I saw a hunger there, a look of frustration. And I had an idea why.

Like all true detectives, Arnold was a relentless hunter at heart. He had two prey in his sights, but he knew he could only claim one of them.

He gestured toward Clay, but spoke to Seth. "You're sure about him?"

"I'm sure."

"You're not filing a complaint against him? Nothing?"

"No. Not yet. At least, not now." Seth regarded his brother. "It's really up to him."

Arnold shook his head and gave a sigh and gave a nod to one of his officers. Handcuffs appeared. Grace realized that they were meant for her. She had a moment of stunned silence, realizing that all her machinations, all the lies she'd told herself about protecting her future, had led to this moment of ruin. Her desperation to secure her dream had ultimately destroyed everything she had with Seth. Right before Arnold and his men led her away, she glanced at Seth, desperately hoping for a last-minute reprieve—but Seth turned away.

The brothers exchanged one long last look. Seth paused as he turned, pressing a hand to his ribs like something inside had shifted wrong. Then he gathered his things and walked away.

I lingered, watching Clay, wondering what would happen to him.

He stood imprisoned in the spotlight, isolated and exposed. He looked small, defeated, his head lowered and shoulders slumped.

The set lights dimmed. The echo of Seth's footsteps faded away. Then there came the faint sound of a door closing, leaving an eerie quiet. Clay's silhouette stood stark against the backdrop of their carefully constructed world—a world he had nearly destroyed. The darkness gathered around him, inching closer, until finally it enveloped him entirely.

50

The grass on the northern edge of Woodlawn was always patchy. The sun hit it harder here and the trees didn't offer much shade. It was the quiet end of the cemetery—where the plots were cheaper, the markers smaller and the visitors fewer.

I spotted her from a distance. Sitting on the bench beside the fresh grave, one gloved hand resting in her lap, the other still curled around a closed umbrella. She wasn't using it. Just holding it like a shield she hadn't raised.

I made my way up the hill, the gravel crunching underfoot. She didn't turn around.

"Sadie."

She looked up then. Not surprised. Just tired.

"I figured you'd come," she said.

"I figured you'd be here."

She nodded once. "They just set the stone yesterday."

The headstone was simple—black granite, small but clean. No photo. No epitaph. Just a name, two dates and beneath them: *He saw it all.*

"He would've liked that," I said.

Sadie gave the faintest smile. "He hated fuss."

I sat down beside her. The breeze lifted a curl of her hair and she let it fall back in place without brushing it aside.

"I promised you I'd tell you what I found," I said.

She didn't move. Just waited.

"It wasn't suicide." I gave her the details.

Her eyes closed for a long moment. A slow breath in. Then out. When she opened them again, they glistened, but no tears fell.

"Someone pushed him?" Her voice was level, but something in it was braced—like she already knew the answer and only needed to hear it said aloud.

I nodded. "Hit him with a pipe. From the catwalk."

She shook her head, bewildered. "Why?" Then had a sudden thought. "Did it have anything to do with what he found in the room?"

"Yeah. It proved something he already suspected. Knowing it put him too close to the truth—closer than someone could allow."

Sadie looked at the marker again.

"Then I wish I'd never show him the room. Never let him in. It's just like I said. It never pays to talk about guests. I should've kept my mouth shut. If I had, he'd still be alive."

"Not necessarily. He was determined. He would've found another way."

I remembered something Mrs. Cardigan once said: "Blame's not a pie, child. Just because you get a slice doesn't mean you get the whole thing."

Sadie smiled at my mention of it.

I went on. "And he would've never met you. You mattered to him. More than you know."

There was one other thing I thought I should tell her.

"The thing he found? He didn't run with it. He waited. Thought maybe—just maybe—it could end another way."

Sadie pressed her lips together. Her fingers tightened around the handle of the umbrella.

"Do they know who did it?"

I nodded. "Yes."

"Will there be a trial?"

"Yes."

"Good."

It was a quiet good. Measured. But it had weight.

We sat there a long time, just looking at the grave. The city hummed somewhere beyond the gates—trolleys groaning, horns calling, the muffled rhythm of a place too busy to grieve.

Finally, she spoke again. "Do you believe in second chances, Lanie?"

I looked down the slope toward the sunlit rows.

"Sometimes," I said. "If you're lucky. If you're willing to fight for it."

She didn't answer. But she reached into her bag and pulled out a small bouquet. White lilies. Clean. Unfussy.

She placed them at the base of the stone and stood. "He was starting to believe in one," she said. "I suppose I should try to do the same."

We didn't say goodbye. Just walked down the hill together, past the rows of the dead, toward the noise of the living.

51

Clay didn't return to the set the next day. Neither did Grace.

Seth stood before of the crew the next morning. His eyes were bloodshot. His clothes hung wrinkled, as though they'd been slept in or not taken off at all. A dry cough escaped him before he could suppress it. He pressed a hand to his chest, as if steadying something deep inside.

The summer rain drummed against the warehouse roof, a slow, steady rhythm and for a long moment, no one spoke.

"Clay won't be returning," Seth finally said. His voice was steady, but the effort it took to keep it that way was visible. "He's, uh ... he's decided to pursue other opportunities." No mention of sabotage, no hint of the ruptured trust that had driven them apart. The crew listened in silence, their faces a mosaic of confusion.

"And Grace..." A shift went through the room. "There's something I need to tell you," he paused. "Grace won't be coming back. She's been taken in—arrested."

He didn't say the word *murder*. He didn't have to. Every

person on that set had loved Westbrook in one way or another. They all knew.

No further explanation. Just the facts. Just enough to confirm what some had begun to suspect and others couldn't yet believe.

A crew member who lingered after wrap claimed he saw her being led away. Someone else said there was a detective on set, that she went quietly. Nobody could say for sure.

A few heads dropped. One woman wiped her cheek with the back of her wrist. Someone in the grip crew cursed under his breath. The air went still.

Seth looked as if he'd aged ten years overnight. "I wish I could explain it," he said. "I wish I understood it myself. I can't tell you what happens next. Not to her. Not to this film. All I know is, we have two weeks left to shoot and I plan to finish. If you want to walk, I'll understand."

Silence met his words. A heavy, fraught silence. Then, one by one, nods. A murmur of assent. Not relief—never relief—but determination. Seth had given them something to hold onto, something to push against the grief.

Still, it wasn't the same. Couldn't be.

When work resumed, it moved slower. The atmosphere wasn't tense. It was bruised.

Filming continued, but the energy had changed. No one cracked jokes between takes anymore. There were no easy smiles, no late-night drinks after wrapping for the day. People moved with a kind of mechanical focus, determined to see the film through but haunted by the reality of what had happened.

The crew had lost something they hadn't even realized they were relying on. Grace had been a pillar—not just a star, but a sign they were doing something bold, something that mattered. Her disappearance created a silence that felt colder than Clay's. And Clay, well—his absence didn't stay a mystery for long. The missed cues, the loose rigging, the flickering lamps—they'd stopped. One week passed. Then another. The set ran clean. Tools stayed put. Lights stayed lit.

Whispers began to move through the warehouse. Quiet realizations shared over meals and cigarette breaks. One person remembered Clay near the catwalk the day a sandbag dropped. Another recalled his odd silence after the grip truck was nearly torched. It didn't take long for the truth to settle in. Clay had been the saboteur.

There was shock. Then a bitter, hollow kind of acceptance. But oddly, there was relief too. As if some weight had lifted from the crew's collective shoulders. The work got easier—not physically, but emotionally. There was less fear, less second-guessing. People looked each other in the eye again.

As for Grace, her absence carried a different kind of heaviness. At first, it felt impossible. People clung to doubts. Then the papers caught up. Lanie's paper printed the headline first. **GRACE CARTER ARRESTED FOR MURDER OF BELOVED FILM VETERAN.** Soon it was everywhere. The *Defender, California Eagle, Pittsburgh Courier.* Even the white dailies joined in, draping the story in scandal: *Starlet Kills Cameraman in Lovers' Quarrel! Behind the Glamour: The Dark Secrets of Race Film's Leading Lady!*

It didn't matter that she hadn't been tried. The damage was done. Crew members fielded questions from neighbors, pastors, cousins. Some offered defenses. Others didn't know what to say. The paper on the bulletin board got torn down, pinned back up, then torn down again.

Seth spoke of neither Grace nor Clay again. His silence held everything: sorrow, disbelief, the last frayed threads of dignity. He rewrote scenes. Rearranged schedules. When someone suggested cutting the project short, he said no. Not with words—with action. He kept filming.

His determination to finish the film never wavered. If anything, it burned brighter, more relentless. The sound of hammers and saws filled the air, accompanied by the faint scent of sawdust and sweat. The crew moved with purpose, their shared goal binding them together even tighter. Every scene shot, every line delivered, was proof of their grit— their refusal to let the worst of this industry destroy them.

The crew followed his lead. The atmosphere wasn't light, but it was steady. They moved like people holding together in a storm, bracing against everything outside.

And in time, the rhythm returned. No more missed cues. No more broken gear. Just the sound of a crew holding together by grit and will, pushing through grief the only way they knew how—by making something out of it.

When the final shot was in the can, Seth gave the signal. He looked at the team he still had—their faces drawn, their bodies tired—and gave them what they'd earned.

"That's a wrap, people."

It should've landed like a victory. Instead, it settled quiet and solemn, like the last line of a eulogy.

There were a few claps. Someone whistled. But mostly, they packed their gear like people closing a chapter they'd written in blood and sweat and silence.

They'd made their film. And though none of them said it aloud, they all knew:

This wasn't the ending they'd imagined. But it was the one they'd survived.

52

The day of the film's release arrived like a long-awaited dawn after an endless night. The streets of Harlem had never felt so alive, thrumming with an electric energy that was almost tangible. Posters for *Soul Redemption* adorned storefronts and lampposts, their bold colors and evocative imagery drawing eyes and sparking conversations.

Inside the theater, the air buzzed with anticipation. The scent of freshly popped corn mingled with the faint mustiness of old velvet seats, creating an atmosphere both nostalgic and new. The audience filled the space, their murmurs blending into a low hum that underscored the tension of the moment.

As the lights dimmed, a hush fell over the crowd, replaced by the flicker of the projector casting its glow onto the screen. Seth stood at the back, his silhouette barely visible, but the intensity in his stance was unmistakable. His fingers twitched slightly, a physical manifestation of the nerves that simmered beneath his composed exterior.

The opening scenes captured the audience from the get-go. They held their breath as the story unfolded—frame after frame, each line delivered with raw emotion. The sound of jazz and spirituals, an integral part of the narrative, wove through the scenes, magnifying the pain and the final victory depicted on the screen.

When the final credits rolled, there was a moment of deep silence, an indication of the film's profound impact. Then the applause erupted, a wave of sound that crashed over the room, shaking the very walls. Faces lit up with genuine smiles, tears glistening in some eyes—an expression of the emotional journey they had just experienced.

Seth stepped forward then, his face illuminated by the glow of the screen. For a moment, he seemed almost ageless, caught in the light of what they'd made. But when he raised a hand to acknowledge the crowd, it trembled slightly. He didn't need words; the pride and satisfaction radiated from him, mirrored in the faces of his crew. They had done it. Against all odds, they had created something beautiful, something true.

I hung around, chatting up people, till the theater had emptied. By then, the crew had scattered to back slaps and whispered plans. I caught sight of Seth standing alone near the edge of the lobby, one hand resting on the wall for balance. No speech, no grand farewell. Just a man watching his work echo into the world, breath slower now, shoulders slack with a fatigue that no rest would fix.

I didn't call out to him. He caught my eye, gave the barest nod, then turned away.

As the reviews poured in, the response was overwhelmingly positive. Critics lauded the film for its authenticity, its depth, its unapologetic celebration of Negro life and culture. Words like "masterpiece" and "revolutionary" were thrown around, cementing *Soul Redemption* place in the canon of race films.

Seth and his crew basked in the validation, relieved and exhilarated. Their hard work had finally found recognition on a grand scale. The sense of accomplishment was palpable. The shared triumph knit them even closer together. They had faced sabotage, doubt and the threat of failure, but now they stood victorious.

And yet, amid the celebration, there was a lingering shadow—the absence of Clay, the brother who should have been part of this victory. It was a bittersweet reminder that success often comes at a cost, that behind the accolades and applause lay the complex, painful truths of human relationships.

But for now, in this moment, they allowed themselves to revel in their achievement. The future could wait. Tonight, they celebrated their resilience, their talent and the indomitable spirit that had carried them through.

53

Months later, the excitement of the film's success gave way to a different kind of anticipation: Seth Carter and *Soul Redemption* were nominated to receive the Black Oscar. No, not a copy made after the Oscar of Hollywood. That came a couple of years later. This was the first Oscar. It was made of onyx and polished to a high gleam. It was named after the leading colored filmmaker of our time —Oscar Micheaux—and it was considered the highest award you could receive in race films.

The Harlem Opera House on West 125th Street was the chosen venue. It was a lovely place. Very grand and regal. It had a wide, sweeping staircase and a balcony of polished Italian marble. The auditorium held more than a thousand seats. They were plush and blue. Three tiers of box seats arose on either side of the stage. They were mighty grand, too, set forward and open, so that those who occupied them could not only see but be seen. Then, there was the stage itself. It was wide and deep and framed by richly velvet curtains.

Despite its name, it had been a long time since the

Harlem Opera House had been used for opera. I'm not sure when the switchover happened. But I do know that up until a couple of years earlier (I think 1922, to be exact), it was part of the vaudeville circuit. Now, it was mainly a jazz venue. As such, it featured some of the leading jazz lights of the day. In short, it was fit for a king, the king of race awards, the Black Oscar.

That night, the theater buzzed with an electric energy. The scent of polished wood mingled with that of freshly pressed suits and delicate floral perfumes. I sat in one of the box seats, enjoying a birds'-eye view of the stage and audience. Looking down at all those talented people, to see them gathered in one place, I felt a surge of pride. My god! And the power of the stories that had brought us here! It was surreal.

My gaze roamed across the room, taking in the familiar faces—Seth, his expression calm but his eyes betraying his nerves; crew members scattered throughout, their camaraderie now a silent support system.

That was when I saw him.

Clay sat at the very back of the theater, half-shrouded in shadow. His wiry frame seemed smaller, more fragile than I remembered. I felt a jolt of surprise, followed by a rush of curiosity. Did Seth know Clay was there? Invited him, perhaps? Did Clay's presence indicate the possibility of a reconciliation? Or had Clay been following his brother's success at a distance? And taken it upon himself to attend the ceremonies, to cheer Seth on or lambast him in bitter silence?

Maybe he felt my gaze. I don't know, but at that moment, as I stared down at him, he suddenly looked up. Our eyes met and for me the hum of the audience faded.

His dark eyes, once so full of intensity, now held something else—an unmistakable mix of shame and regret. He didn't flinch or look away. Instead, he held my gaze. The lines on his face seemed deeper, as if etched by the burden of exile and the passage of time.

I felt a pang of empathy, seeing him like this. Our silent exchange lasted mere seconds, yet it conveyed everything unsaid, everything lost. I wanted to speak to him, find out how he was doing, what he was doing. But there was no time to get out of my seat and hurry downstairs to speak with him, not before the ceremonies began. It also wasn't clear whether he'd even speak to me, the person who'd revealed his betrayal.

The houselights dimmed, the stage lights came up and his face fell in shadow. Meanwhile, the music began, an inspiring piece that called to mind images of heroism in the face of likely overwhelming defeat. The presenters appeared, one after the other and winners were announced, each taking to the stage to thrilling applause, each making brief comments that thanked those who had worked with them, supported them, been loyal to them even when others doubted.

Every now and then I looked back to where I'd seen Clay to see if he was there. It was hard to tell.

Then the audience burst into thunderous applause. My gaze shifted back to the stage. Oscar Micheaux himself stood behind the podium. There had been talk—no more than hopeful gossip, really—that Micheaux himself might attend the ceremonies. But no one had believed, had dared believe that—

People jumped to their feet, clapping enthusiastically.

Micheaux made brief and humble but witty remarks, then began to read the lift of nominees for Best Picture. There was a collective holding of breath as he tore open the envelope and held up the small card bearing the winner's name. Reading it, he smiled. And gave a brief nod. For the winner, that flash of approval from the master himself would mean as much, if not more, than receiving the onyx statue.

Micheaux looked out over the audience. He leaned forward to the microphone. The audience fell into a hush. It was the last award of the evening, the one everyone had been waiting for. Micheaux's voice rang out over the auditorium.

"And the winner is ... *Soul Redemption* by Seth Carter!"

The room erupted in applause, clapping hands and whistles of approval. A spotlight swerved to pick out Seth as he rose from his seat, his face alight with surprise, relief and joy. His tall frame moved with elegant resolve as he made his way down the aisle toward center stage. Each step he took was met with admiration, respect. But when he reached the foot of the stairs, he paused, just slightly winded. One hand brushed his side. Then he straightened and climbed.

Micheaux welcomed Seth onstage with a brief hug and a pat on the back, then presented him with the gleaming black statuette that was his well-deserved prize.

Seth's speech was brief but poignant. He thanked the cast and crew, his voice steady yet brimming with emotion. And he mentioned Clay. At the mention of his brother's name, a collective breath seemed to hold within the room.

"I wish my brother could be here tonight," Seth said. "Clay's contribution—not only to *Soul Redemption* but to all my work—was profound." Seth's speech was eloquent, acknowledging everyone who contributed to the film. But his voice faltered when he mentioned Clay, a momentary crack revealing his true feelings. It was a blend of triumph and a subtle sadness, a reflection of the complicated path that had led him to this moment. The applause swelled, rousing and heartfelt, celebrating a victory that was as much about resilience as it was about talent. But Seth's gaze remained distant, locked in a private battle, perhaps seeking one particular face.

Spotlights crisscrossed the audience. For a brief second, one illuminated Clay. His face was pale, almost ghostly. He was standing—

As always, on the outer edge of his brother's glory, overlooked and overshadowed.

Maybe so, but Clay's applause was among the most fervent. His face showed both pride and regret. Our eyes locked again and I saw it—the battle inside him, the remorse for what he had done and the pride in his brother's achievement. It was a complex cocktail of emotions that needed no words to be understood.

My gaze returned to the stage, where Seth stood tall, soaking in the acclaim. When I looked back to Clay once more, I found his seat empty. He had slipped away, silent and unnoticed, a ghost retreating into the shadows. For me, the mood turned somber despite the ongoing celebration. *Perhaps*, I thought hopefully, *he'll meet with Seth later, privately.*

My thoughts returned to a conversation I'd had with Seth after Clay's departure.

For the most part, Seth wouldn't speak about his brother. He wouldn't say, for example, if he knew where Clay had gone or whether the two of them were to stay in contact. However, when I stopped by on that last day of filming, I found Seth in a thoughtful mood. He mentioned a conversation he'd had with Clay. He didn't say when it occurred but it must've been soon after that final confrontation.

"I asked him why—why did he do it? The *real* reason. It couldn't have been just about the money, or even some crazy idea about saving us. There had to have been more to it."

"And what did he tell you?"

Seth shrugged, looking bewildered as if he still couldn't fathom his brother's response, as if it still didn't make sense to him. "All he said was that he'd never felt appreciated. Not just now with this film, but from way back." Seth paused, frowning in thought. "When he said that, I started thinking, remembering how it was when we were kids. He struggled even then. He felt that our folks were always comparing him to me and that he didn't measure up. But that was the crazy thing. He did measure up. He more than measured up. It's just that we had different talents. He's an incredible screenwriter and editor. And he has a knack with technical aspects of filmmaking, too. I can't tell you how rare that is. Usually, it's one or the other."

Seth rubbed his chin. "You know ... Clay was always there for me. Maybe, he was right. Maybe, I did take him for granted. But ..." His voice trailed off. "We were a team, making movies together. It's how I always envisioned it. And now I-I knew he wanted financial stability, that it was important to him and that he wanted recognition, but I guess I just didn't realize how deep his frustrations went. So, I asked him. Why? Why didn't he just tell me how unhappy he was? Why do all that instead of coming to me, talking to me?"

"And what did he say?"

"Well," Seth gave a sad smile. "I must say he let me have it. Right between the eyes. No holds barred. About my ego. My naiveté. And how I was putting my dream above everything else, *everyone* else, to the point of putting people in danger. The proof, he said, was that I did not shut down the film, but kept going—even when the sabotage nearly got people killed."

"Sounds like he knew how to lay on the guilt, to make you feel guilty for what he did."

"True. But he had a point. I was, in fact, taking a big risk, endangering everyone, not just him and me, but our crew, the people who stuck with us through thick and thin, who depended on us for a living. And, to be fair, Clay was also tough on himself. He said he could barely admit his frustration and anger, his resentment, to himself. That it felt like disloyalty, like blasphemy."

I raised an eyebrow. "Blasphemy?"

"Yeah," Seth nodded. "He actually used that word—blasphemy, as if I was a god or something that he was duty-bound to follow, to *worship*. I nearly laughed out loud at that one. But then, he told me something that sobered me up quick.

"He said he'd tried to talk to me. More than once, he'd tried. But I was always so caught up in my dream—*my* dream, mind you, not ours—and so sure of myself, that I wouldn't listen. His exact words—and I'll always remember them—were, 'There was no room for my doubts or fears.' Man, those words cut me to the quick. They sure did. Because I knew they were true."

He paused to catch his breath, pressing a hand to his chest before continuing, quieter now. "What Clay did—I'm not excusing him, no—but what he did wasn't just his fault. It was partly mine, too."

Seth didn't ask me to keep our conversation private. He knew he didn't have to.

And now, once again, Clay had slipped away into the

night. I thought of the camaraderie I'd witnessed on set, the shared vision, the laughter and the challenges. Clay's actions had betrayed not just himself but everyone and he paid a hefty price for it, one that he was perhaps only now beginning to comprehend.

The loss was both personal and communal, a painful reminder of what might have been. The brothers' estrangement felt like a tear in the very fabric of Harlem, a community for which unity and strength weren't luxuries but necessities for survival.

The evening wore on, filled with congratulations, laughter and the occasional tear. Yet, the empty chair at the back of the theater remained a haunting presence. Clay had vanished into the darkness, leaving behind questions and regrets.

The theater buzzed with excitement, but to those who knew the truth behind the glory, it was bittersweet. Seth's face, illuminated by the stage lights, betrayed glimpses of turmoil beneath his composed exterior. His eyes, despite their sparkle, reflected deep sorrow—a brother's absence that no applause could fill.

As he cradled the award, his grip tightened, knuckles pearling. The audience saw a victorious filmmaker; I saw a man grappling with the cost of his success. Seth, for all his ambition and drive, was now more isolated than ever, burdened by the knowledge that he couldn't save his brother, couldn't save his marriage.

And that made me think about my own life, about the lines we draw and the lines we cross when we're desperate to hold on to our dreams. Seth and I, we'd both wanted to believe that dreams could hold a family together. But in the end, it wasn't the dream that undid us—it was the silence, the secrets and the truths we refused to listen to.

54

The townhouse was dark when I let myself in.

I dropped my keys into the dish by the door and stood there a moment, the faint scent of lemon polish still clinging to the air. The old wood of the floor creaked softly beneath my heels, a sound I knew so well I hardly heard it anymore. Tonight, though, it felt different.

The house didn't feel heavy the way it used to.

It didn't feel sacred, either.

It just ... waited.

I wandered into the front parlor. The Chesterfield sofa sat in its usual place, worn at the arms where Hamp's elbow used to rest, but the worn leather seemed to invite rather than accuse. The sideboard caught a sliver of streetlight from between the curtains. Its surface was empty except for a small crystal bowl and a framed photograph.

I crossed to the sofa and rested my hand lightly on the back. The leather felt familiar, comforting, the way it should. I stayed there, not clinging, just ... touching.

No voices echoed here anymore. No ghosts of a painful past—or lost future—whispered from the shadows.

Just silence. Clean and plain. Waiting for whatever I chose to bring into it.

For the first time, I realized the house hadn't been holding me here.

I had been holding myself.

I let out a breath I hadn't known I was holding, picked up the photograph of Hamp, reframed now and smiled— not the kind of smile you wear at funerals, but something smaller, warmer, closer to real.

Then I set the frame back down and went upstairs, the steps under my feet no heavier than they had to be.

55

After Mrs. C left, the house felt lonely and still. I stood by my parlor window, staring out at nothing and everything at once. A saxophone wailed somewhere down the street, slow and low. A tune full of longing that curled through the warm summer night.

Hamp had tried to tell me and I hadn't been able to hear him.
Much like Seth and Clay.

The parallel hit me square in the chest. Seth and Clay. The filmmaker so consumed by his vision he couldn't see his brother slipping away. The resentment building like pressure in a pipe until it finally burst.

I'd covered their story. Written about one brother betraying another. Now here I was, on the verge of making the same mistake.

Sam. Patient Sam who'd offered his key weeks ago. Who'd asked for nothing but kept showing up anyway. And me, keeping him at arm's length because I was too afraid to admit Hamp wasn't coming back.

Mrs. C's petunias and marigolds scented the breeze that stirred the curtains. Her words came back, sharp and clear:

"Moving forward doesn't mean forgetting. It means having the guts to love again."

I drifted to the small dish near the front door. The spare key lay there, untouched since Hamp's funeral. Just metal and teeth, but it might as well have been my heart laid bare.

I reached for it, hesitated, then picked it up and turned it over in my palm. The metal was smooth, warm from the summer air, familiar.

No more waiting. No more hiding.

My fingers curled around it.

It was time.

56

The sharp clink of silverware against china cut through the silence in my townhouse. City noise filtered in from outside, distant and muffled. The aroma of roasted herbs and garlic filled the room.

Sam took a bite, paused with his fork halfway to his mouth. His eyes widened. "Whoa! What happened? This is fabulous."

"Mrs. C's been giving me lessons. She helped me make it."

"Well, I'll be."

Sam's laughter broke the tension. A welcome sound. For weeks, we'd been caught in a professional tailspin. The professional storm had finally passed. We'd finally weathered it. But the personal wreckage? That remained. It needed fixing.

I took a sip of wine. "I've been thinking."

Sam's eyebrow arched. "About?"

I set the glass down. "About Seth and Clay. About how they couldn't hear each other. And about me ... and Hamp."

Sam waited. His shoulders tensed.

"I now see that I've been angry at Hamp for leaving me, for not telling me about his heart condition. But when I think back, I realize he tried. Like Clay, Hamp tried, in his own way, to tell me. And like Seth, I ... I didn't listen." I looked away from Sam's gaze. "I didn't want to."

The ticking of the clock on the mantel filled the silence. I forced myself to meet Sam's eyes.

"All right, Lanie. I get that. We all miss things we're not ready to see. But what I don't get is why you invited me over tonight. It's a lovely meal and all, but ..."

"Does there have to be a reason?"

"Given what's happened between us, I'd say, 'Yes.'"

I tried to smile, faltered. "Gee, you're not going to make this easy for me, are you?"

The corner of Sam's mouth twitched slightly. "No, I'm not. You haven't been making it easy for me. Just giving you a dose of your own medicine."

"Fair enough." I folded my napkin, laid it beside my plate. "I've reached a decision." I glanced up.

Sam put his fork down. The humor vanished from his eyes. "And that would be?"

The words caught in my throat. Outside, a car horn blared. My heart pounded, reminding me how fragile life could be, how quickly everything could change.

I walked to the hutch, retrieved the small blue velvet box I'd placed there earlier. Returned to Sam and placed it on the table between us.

A hint of *Acqua di Parma* drifted past. Hamp's cologne. For a moment, I felt him there. Approval in his absence.

I slid the box across the table. "It's the key to my townhouse."

Sam didn't move. His hands stayed in his lap. I couldn't tell if he was surprised, or maybe just cautious, but his eyes betrayed feelings more complicated than I'd expected.

"You're sure?"

"Yes. I've thought about it. And I want you to have it."

He moved his hand toward the box but stopped.

"Please, Sam."

He opened the box. The silver key gleamed in the soft light. He took it out, heft it in his palm. It was a big key, but it looked small in his large hands.

Just as it had in Hamp's.

"Was this his, Lanie?"

I couldn't speak. Just nodded.

Sam went still. The silence in the room deepened as he stared at the key. This wasn't just any key—it was Hamp's. The physical token of another man's place in my life, in my home.

"You're giving me Hamp's key." Not a question. A statement.

I found my voice. "Yes."

Sam's eyes met mine. "That's not a small thing."

"I know."

He turned the key over once more. "I understand what this means, Lanie. What you're letting go of."

The depth in his voice caught me off guard. Sam had never met Hamp, but in that moment, I felt he understood exactly what this gesture cost me.

After a long moment, he placed the key flat on the table. "But I have to ask—are you sure you're doing this for the right reasons? Not out of fear?"

"Fear? I don't understand."

"You're scared. We had a fight. Two fights, in fact. One in our professional life and one in our personal one. In the first, you stood up to me. But now, I feel that you're backing down. Because you don't trust me."

"Oh, Sam, no! It's not like that at all."

"Then how is it?" His eyes searched my face. "Are you sure this is what you want? Or are you just doing this because you're afraid of losing someone again?"

The question caught me off-guard.

"I'm not saying no," he added, voice softening. "But I need to know if you're ready. Really ready. Not just scared of repeating the past."

The certainty in Sam's eyes had given way to something I rarely saw there. Doubt.

"I don't want to lose you," I admitted. "And yes, I want to move forward. Not let Hamp's memory hold me back anymore."

Sam turned the key over in his hand. After a long moment, he sighed and met my gaze.

"You were right before, Lanie. About me. About how I keep things close to the vest." He tapped the key against his palm. "You called me out on it and I bit back hard. Too hard."

His admission surprised me. Sam wasn't one to backtrack.

"There are things in my past I haven't told you," he continued. "Things I've been... protecting you from. Or maybe protecting myself from having to face again." He shook his head slightly. "And that wasn't fair. Not when I'm asking you to be open with me."

I reached across the table, touched his hand. "Sam—"

"No, let me finish. I understand that this is also why you've been hesitant. How can you fully trust someone who doesn't trust you enough to share their whole self?" The lines around his eyes deepened. "I will tell you. When the time is right. But I want you to know I'm working on it."

I saw then that we mirrored each other. Both afraid. Both holding tight to our secrets—me to Hamp's memory, him to his unshared history.

"I understand that you're still testing the waters," he said, "whether you can let yourself dive all the way in. One step at a time. We don't have to figure it all out tonight."

I felt grateful for his patience. This wasn't just about the key—it was about trust we were still building, cracks that needed mending.

Sam slipped the key onto his keyring. The sound of metal against metal felt final somehow.

"I'll take it. But this isn't about the key. It's about what that key represents. And that's something we still have to figure out."

The breath I'd been holding left in a rush. His words settled between us, a promise we still had to honor.

Sam reached across the table and took my hand. "We'll figure it out. Together."

He stood, pulling me up from the table and into his arms. The warmth of his embrace melted the last of my nerves and I rested my head against his chest, letting the steady beat of his heart ground me.

"I'm not going anywhere," he murmured against my hair. "And neither are you."

I closed my eyes, letting the moment stretch out between us. There was still so much we hadn't said, so much we hadn't figured out. But tonight, it didn't feel so daunting. We didn't need all the answers right now. We just needed to keep moving forward, one step at a time.

57

*S*oul Redemption became a classic. It also turned out to be Seth's last film. He was gone six months later. Tuberculosis. He was thirty-four. When I learned of his illness, I thought back, piecing together moments from my memory, each one gaining a new, painful clarity. I could still hear Clay's words—"and how we'd spend his money when he's gone."

The words had struck me as particularly callous, even made me wonder whether Clay and Grace had been contemplating murder. I'd dismissed those suspicions in light of his exile and her imprisonment, but now they came rushing back. *When he's gone.*

And then there were Grace's words defending her killing of Westbrook: "I did it for the both of us, hon. He was going to tell on us. I told him the news would kill you. But he didn't want to listen. He just kept saying that a man in your state had a right to know."

A man in your state.

So not only Clay and Grace but Westbrook had known. They'd all known. That Seth was ill, probably dying and that *Soul Redemption* would likely be his last film. Seth had fought valiantly to complete it and both his wife and his brother done everything to obstruct him.

Thinking back, I realized how many of Seth's words, his urgency, had masked a deeper fear—a fear that he was running out of time. While in the hospital, confronting the prospect of imminent death, Seth continued to work, maybe with the hope that someone would pick up his projects when he was gone—or maybe just because a creative mind doesn't stop, until it stops. His work consumed him, even when everything else fell away.

He was laboring over a script when I visited him in the hospital. He admitted to struggling with it.

"I still think of Grace when I write the part for my leading lady. This script? It'll never be as good as it would've been if Grace and Clay had been here working on it with me."

He didn't say it, but I could read the question in his eyes. *Was I wrong to have sent him away? Shouldn't I have forgiven him and just let it go?*

A week later he was gone. Thousands of fans packed the church where his services were held and Micheaux himself delivered the eulogy. It was a bright balmy spring day. I think Seth would've been especially pleased with the weather. It was neither too hot nor too cold; the perfect temperature and the perfect light for outdoor shooting.

In fact, the weather that spring had been so kind that trees at Woodlawn Cemetery were in full bloom already—their leaves thick enough to cast a shadow, one a man could hide in

I first spotted him during the prayers at the graveyard. He was standing off to one side. When the crowd dispersed, he came forward to stand at the still-open grave.

It was Clay. He was reed thin. He looked down at Seth's casket, as if trying to speak to a brother who couldn't answer him anymore.

I wondered whether he would speak with me, but I needn't have worried. When I approached him, he was cordial. I asked him what he was doing, but he wouldn't say. Instead, he glanced down at the casket, the grief raw in his voice.

"I managed to see him once, you know. At the hospital, just before the end. We didn't say much, but we said enough." He took a breath, steadying himself. "He told me he forgave me. And maybe... maybe I forgave him, too. At least, I'd like to think I did."

After a pause, he straightened up and forced a tight smile. "I used to blame you for what happened to me. There was a time when I would've..." His voice trailed off.

"Wrung my neck?"

He gave a wry smile. "Yes, actually. That describes it perfectly." He paused. "Let's just say I'm better now. I know it wasn't your fault; it was mine. I made my bed and I'll lie in it till the day I die."

He didn't wait for me to respond. He nodded instead, a strange mixture of resignation and relief in his eyes, then turned and walked away, shoulders hunched under a burden he would carry to the end of his days. This wasn't the same Clay Seth had banished from his set, from his life. That Clay had been defiant, unwilling to face his own failings. This Clay was gaunt with remorse, steeped in self-condemnation.

Forgiveness and regret—two specters that haunt both the living and the dead. His figure slowly dissolved into the shadows of the cemetery. I wanted to call after him, to tell him something—anything—but what could I say? That his grief, raw and unguarded, meant more than any apology? That yes, being forgiven by the person you've hurt can sometimes feel hollow, especially when you can't forgive yourself?

I could've said those things. Maybe more. Maybe the most important thing of all—that Seth had always believed in Clay's talent, even at the end.

But what good would it have done?

In their final moments together, a dying Seth and a broken Clay had spoken their truths, offering each other absolution. It had no doubt eased their pain, but it wasn't enough to heal the wounds they'd suffered. Only time together might have done that—but time was something they'd run out of.

Maybe forgiveness isn't about breaking free of the past. Maybe it's just about loosening the grip it has on you, for however long you have left.

But if that's the case, it only worked for Seth.

Clay remained a man haunted, shackled to a past he couldn't escape. He disappeared into obscurity after that and, to my knowledge, no one in the race film industry ever saw or heard from him again.

EPILOGUE

Seth and Clay. Two brothers who loved each other. They didn't set out to destroy one another. They started out with the same dream, the same fire and somewhere along the line, they lost sight of each other. They thought they had time, that they could make up for the missed chances, the unspoken resentments and eventual regrets. But time has a way of running out on you, just when you think you've got it all under control.

Seth wanted to make something that lasted. He had a vision and he chased it so hard, he couldn't see that he was leaving Clay behind, one step at a time. And Clay—well, he thought he could swallow his pride, bury his fear and frustration, pretend it didn't matter. Until it did.

By then, the damage was done. And dreams? They don't mean much when the ground beneath them is cracked wide open. When the person who was supposed to be standing by you is the very person you had to send away.

You can look back, try to piece together where it all went wrong. But some things, once broken, just can't be put back together. And some losses—they stay with you, no matter how much you wish you could turn back the clock.

It's not always the big things that break you. Sometimes, it's the silence. The things you never said and the things you never saw, until it's too late.

ABOUT THE AUTHOR

"Just the facts, ma'am. Just the facts."

Persia Walker writes critically-acclaimed 1920s crime novels. A native New Yorker, she has lived in Germany, Brazil, Poland and France.

Her online home is PersiaWalker.com. You can connect with her there or on Facebook.

ALSO BY PERSIA WALKER

Have you read the others?

THE LANIE PRICE SERIES

Goodfellowe House

Black Orchid Blues

Backdrop to Murder

Dear Sister Dead

STANDALONES

Lyrics of a Blackbird

www.ingramcontent.com/pod-product-compliance
Lightning Source LLC
Chambersburg PA
CBHW031600240626
47153CB00002B/587